STUDY GUIDE

Ethan Frome

Edith Wharton

WITH CONNECTIONS

HOLT, RINEHART AND WINSTON

A Harcourt Classroom Education Company

Austin • New York • Orlando • Atlanta • San Francisco • Boston • Dallas • Toronto • London

Staff Credits

Associate Director: Kathleen Daniel

Managing Editor: Mike Topp

Manager of Editorial Services: Abigail Winograd

Editorial: Catherine Goodridge

Writer: Mairead Stack

Editorial Staff: *Assistant Managing Editor,* Elizabeth LaManna; *Copyediting Manager,* Robert Kelly; *Senior Copyeditors,* John Haffner Layden, Leora Harris; *Copyeditors,* Julie Brye, Edward S. Cohen, James Erdman, Sacha Frey, Tamsin Nutter, Nancy Shore; *Editorial Operations Coordinators,* Meredith Goldfarb, David Smith; *Support,* Adam Jaquette, Kristin Wodarski; *Senior Word Processor,* Laurie Muir, *Word Processor,* Louise Fernandez

Permissions: Jonathan Kauffman, Lee Noble

Design: Betty Mintz and Joseph Padial

Prepress Production: Carol Marunas

Manufacturing Coordinator: Athena Blackorby

Cover Illustration: *Mountain Winter.* Woodcut (15" x 10") ©1979 Sabra Field.

ISBN 0-03-056481-6

1 2 3 4 5 6   085   02 01 00

TABLE *of* CONTENTS

Using This Study Guide

Approaching the Novel

The successful study of a novel often depends on students' enthusiasm, curiosity, and openness. The ideas in **Introducing the Novel** will help you create such a climate for your class. Background information in **About the Writer** and **About the Novel** can also be used to pique students' interest.

Reading and Responding to the Novel

Making Meanings questions are designed for both individual response and group or class discussion. They range from personal response to high-level critical thinking.

Reading Strategies worksheets contain graphic organizers. They help students explore techniques that enhance both comprehension and literary analysis. Many worksheets are appropriate for more than one set of chapters.

Novel Notes provide high-interest information relating to historical, cultural, literary, and other elements of the novel. The **Investigate** questions and **Reader's Log** ideas guide students to further research and consideration.

Choices suggest a wide variety of activities for exploring different aspects of the novel, either individually or collaboratively. The results may be included in a portfolio or used as springboards for larger projects.

The **Glossary and Vocabulary** list (1) clarifies allusions and other references and (2) provides definitions students may refer to as they read. The **Vocabulary Worksheets** activities are based on the Vocabulary Words.

Reader's Log, Double-Entry Journal, and **Group Discussion Log** model formats and spark ideas for responding to the novel. These pages are designed to be a resource for independent reading as well.

Responding to the Novel as a Whole

The following features provide options for culminating activities that can be used in whole-class, small-group, or independent-study situations.

Novel Review provides a format for summarizing and integrating the major literary elements.

Novel Projects suggest multiple options for culminating activities. **Writing About the Novel, Cross-Curricular Connections,** and **Multimedia and Internet Connections** propose project options that extend the text into other genres, content areas, and environments.

Responding to the Connections

Making Meanings questions in **Exploring the Connections** facilitate discussion of the additional readings in the HRW LIBRARY edition of this novel.

This Study Guide is intended to

- *provide maximum versatility and flexibility*
- *serve as a ready resource for background information on both the author and the book*
- *act as a catalyst for discussion, analysis, interpretation, activities, and further research*
- *provide reproducible masters that can be used for either individual or collaborative work, including discussions and projects*
- *provide multiple options for evaluating students' progress through the novel and the Connections*

Literary Elements

- plot structure
- major themes
- characterization
- setting
- point of view
- symbolism, irony, and other elements appropriate to the title

Making Meanings Reproducible Masters

- First Thoughts
- Shaping Interpretations
- Connecting with the Text
- Extending the Text
- Challenging the Text

A **Reading Check** focuses on review and comprehension.

The Worksheets Reproducible Masters

- Reading Strategies Worksheets
- Literary Elements Worksheets
- Vocabulary Worksheets

Reaching All Students

Most classrooms include students from a variety of backgrounds and with a range of learning styles. The questions and activities in this Study Guide have been developed to meet diverse student interests, abilities, and learning styles. Of course, students are full of surprises, and a question or activity that is challenging to an advanced student can also be handled successfully by students who are less proficient readers. The interest level, flexibility, and variety of these questions and activities make them appropriate for a range of students.

Struggling Readers and Students with Limited English Proficiency: The **Making Meanings** questions, the **Choices** activities, and the **Reading Strategies** worksheets all provide opportunities for students to check their understanding of the text and to review their reading. The **Novel Projects** ideas are designed for a range of student abilities and learning styles. Both questions and activities motivate and encourage students to make connections to their own interests and experiences. The **Vocabulary Worksheets** can be used to facilitate language acquisition. **Dialogue Journals**, with you the teacher or with more advanced students as respondents, can be especially helpful to these students.

Advanced Students: The writing opportunity suggested with the **Making Meanings** questions and the additional research suggestions in **Novel Notes** should offer a challenge to these students. The **Choices** and **Novel Projects** activities can be taken to advanced levels. **Dialogue Journals** allow advanced students to act as mentors or to engage each other intellectually.

Auditory Learners: A range of suggestions in this Study Guide targets students who respond particularly well to auditory stimuli: making and listening to audiotapes and engaging in class discussion, role-playing, debate, oral reading, and oral presentation. See **Making Meanings** questions, **Choices**, and **Novel Projects** options (especially **Cross-Curricular Connections** and **Multimedia and Internet Connections**).

Visual/Spatial Learners: Students are guided to create visual representations of text scenes and concepts and to analyze films or videos in **Choices** and in **Novel Projects**. The **Reading Strategies** and **Literary Elements Worksheets** utilize graphic organizers as a way to both assimilate and express information.

Tactile/Kinesthetic Learners: The numerous interactive, hands-on, and problem-solving projects are designed to encourage the involvement of students motivated by action and movement. The projects also provide an opportunity for **interpersonal learners** to connect with others through novel-related tasks. The **Group Discussion Log** will help students track the significant points of their interactions.

Verbal Learners: For students who naturally connect to the written and spoken word, the **Reader's Logs** and **Dialogue Journals** will have particular appeal. This Study Guide offers numerous writing opportunities: See **Making Meanings, Choices, Novel Notes,** and **Writing About the Novel** in **Novel Projects**. These options should also be attractive to **intrapersonal learners**.

Assessment Options

Perhaps the most important goal of assessment is to provide feedback on the effectiveness of instructional strategies. As you monitor the degree to which your students understand and engage with the novel, you will naturally adjust the frequency and ratio of class to small-group and verbal to nonverbal activities, as well as the extent to which direct teaching of reading strategies, literary elements, or vocabulary is appropriate to your students' needs.

If you are in an environment where **portfolios** contain only carefully chosen samples of students' writing, you may want to introduce a second, "working," portfolio and negotiate grades with students after examining all or selected items from this portfolio.

The features in this Study Guide are designed to facilitate a variety of assessment techniques.

Reader's Logs and Double-Entry Journals can be briefly reviewed and responded to (students may wish to indicate entries they would prefer to keep private). The logs and journals are an excellent measure of students' engagement with and understanding of the novel.

Group Discussion Log entries provide students with an opportunity for self-evaluation of their participation in both novel discussions and project planning.

Making Meanings questions allow you to observe and evaluate a range of student responses. Those who have difficulty with literal and interpretive questions may respond more completely to **Connecting** and **Extending**. The **Writing Opportunity** provides you with the option of ongoing assessment: You can provide feedback to students' brief written responses to these prompts as they progress through the novel.

Reading Strategies Worksheets, Novel Review, and Literary Elements Worksheets lend themselves well to both quick assessment and students' self-evaluation. They can be completed collaboratively and the results shared with the class, or students can compare their individual responses in a small-group environment.

Choices activities and writing prompts offer all students the chance to successfully complete an activity, either individually or collaboratively, and share the results with the class. These items are ideal for peer evaluation and can help prepare students for presenting and evaluating larger projects at the completion of the novel unit.

Vocabulary Worksheets can be used as diagnostic tools or as part of a concluding test.

Novel Projects evaluations might be based on the degree of understanding of the novel demonstrated by the project. Students' presentations of their projects should be taken into account, and both self-evaluation and peer evaluation can enter into the overall assessment.

The **Test** is a traditional assessment tool in three parts: objective items, short-answer questions, and essay questions.

Questions for Self-evaluation and Goal Setting

- What are the three most important things I learned in my work with this novel?
- How will I follow up so that I remember them?
- What was the most difficult part of working with this novel?
- How did I deal with the difficulty, and what would I do differently?
- What two goals will I work toward in my reading, writing, group, and other work?
- What steps will I take to achieve those goals?

Items for a "Working" Portfolio

- reading records
- drafts of written work and project plans
- audio- and videotapes of presentations
- notes on discussions
- reminders of cooperative projects, such as planning and discussion notes
- artwork
- objects and mementos connected with themes and topics in the novel
- other evidence of engagement with the novel

For help with establishing and maintaining portfolio assessment, examine the **Portfolio Management System** *in* ELEMENTS OF LITERATURE.

Answer Key

The Answer Key at the back of this guide is not intended to be definitive or to set up a right-wrong dichotomy. In questions that involve interpretation, however, students' responses should be defended by citations from the text.

About the Writer

More on Wharton

Ammons, Elizabeth. *Edith Wharton's Argument with America.* Athens, GA: University of Georgia Press, 1980.

Auchincloss, Louis. *Edith Wharton: A Woman in Her Time.* New York: Viking, 1971.

Lewis, R.W.B. *Edith Wharton: A Biography.* New York: Harper & Row, 1975.

Raphael, Lev. *Edith Wharton's Prisoners of Shame: A New Perspective on Her Neglected Fiction.* New York: St. Martin's Press, 1991.

Springer, Marlene. *Ethan Frome: A Nightmare of Need.* New York: Twayne, 1993.

Wolff, Cynthia Griffin. *A Feast of Words: The Triumph of Edith Wharton.* Reading, MA: Addison-Wesley, 1995.

Also by Wharton

Fiction

The House of Mirth (1905)

The Custom of the Country (1913)

Summer (1917)

The Age of Innocence (1920)

The Buccaneers (1938) unfinished

Memoir

A Backward Glance (1934)

A biography of Edith Wharton appears in Ethan Frome, HRW LIBRARY *edition. You may wish to share this additional biographical information with your students.*

Edith Newbold Jones Wharton was born into a wealthy and socially prominent New York family in 1862. When she was four years old, the family moved to Europe. During their six-year stay there she contracted a severe case of typhoid fever, presaging bouts of illness that were to recur throughout her life. Educated at home by private tutors, Edith showed an early interest in writing, and her mother had a book of her daughter's verses published when the girl was just sixteen. As a young woman, she took part in the social round expected of girls of her class. In 1883, she met two men who were to play key roles in her emotional life. The first, Walter Berry, became a lifelong friend and trusted confidant. The other, Edward (Teddy) Wharton, she married in 1885 and divorced twenty-eight years later.

The marriage appears to have been unsatisfying from the start. Teddy was an idle sportsman, living on both his and Edith's inherited wealth. He had little appreciation for her intellectual gifts or independent spirit. They did share a love of travel, and in the early years of their marriage they made frequent journeys between New York, Newport, and Europe. During those years, Edith continued writing, publishing short stories, a book on interior decoration, and a long historical novel. She was often depressed and suffered from unexplained exhaustion and nausea. In 1901, she decided that she needed a permanent home and built the Mount, a mansion in Lenox, Massachusetts, where she lived, wrote, and entertained for the next ten years. She achieved her first major critical and popular success in 1905 with *The House of Mirth,* a novel set in the wealthy New York social circles she knew so well.

Her health improved during those years, but Teddy's declined, and the couple began spending winters in Paris, where Edith wrote a sketch in French that she later developed into *Ethan Frome.* She found increasing satisfaction in her writing and in her friendships, including a somewhat competitive relationship with the novelist Henry James. At the same time her marriage was deteriorating. Teddy had embezzled money from her and spent it on another woman. He was dissolute, abusive, and mentally unstable. At times he required nursing care, which Edith felt it was her duty to provide. Eventually she took bold steps for a middle-aged woman of her time and background: She took up residence in Paris alone, had a love affair with a dashing American journalist, Morton Fullerton, and eventually divorced her husband despite strong social disapproval. Her affair with Fullerton ended painfully after three years, but it did give Wharton what may have been her only experience of passionate love.

Now independent in every sense of the word, Wharton continued to write both fiction and nonfiction and to travel widely with Walter Berry and other good friends. During World War I, she energetically organized huge war-relief efforts. In 1921, she was awarded the Pulitzer Prize for her novel *The Age of Innocence,* an unflinching look into the morals and mores of New York society.

When Walter Berry died, in 1927, Wharton became desolate. He had been an old and valued friend. She published a memoir, *A Backward Glance,* in 1934 and was writing another novel, *The Buccaneers,* when she died of a stroke, in August of 1937. She was buried at Versailles, in France, next to the ashes of her beloved friend Walter Berry.

About the Novel

Special Considerations

Possible sensitive issues in this novel are the bleak and uncompromising tone and ending, the negative portrayal of marriage, the love of a married man for a woman who is not his wife, and the belief by two of the characters that suicide is the only escape open to them.

For Viewing

Ethan Frome. Buena Vista Films, 1992. PG. Directed by John Madden, this production stars Patricia Arquette.

For Listening

Ethan Frome. DhAudio, 1992. A dramatization of the novel.

Ethan Frome. Naxos AudioBooks, 1993. An abridged version narrated by Richard Thomas.

Historical Context

When Ethan Frome was published, in 1911, some reviewers and readers were disappointed by, and even critical of, its rural setting and working-class characters. They thought of Edith Wharton as an accomplished writer of novels of manners, and they expected her to continue to focus on those circles of upper-class society in which she moved. What could she know of the life of poor farmers like Ethan Frome? Edith Wharton answered those charges in her introduction to the 1922 edition of the novel and in her memoir, *A Backward Glance,* where she asserted that *Ethan Frome* "was written after [she] had spent ten years in the hill-region [near her Berkshire mansion] where the scene is laid, during which years [she] had come to know well the aspect, dialect, and mental and moral attitude of the hill-people."*

The main events of the novel take place in rural New England in the 1880s, a generation earlier than Wharton's residence in the area, yet research bears out the accuracy of the social and economic portrait she painted. In the late nineteenth century, farming the rocky New England soil was indeed a life of backbreaking labor for meager reward. Many young men chose to abandon the land for work in the cities, or some ventured west in search of greater opportunities. Life for farm women was even grimmer. Along with their husbands they experienced poverty and daily drudgery, but more than their husbands, they were isolated and housebound (without radio, telephone, or automobile). Eventually even the medical establishment began taking notice of their plight, as indicated by a 1913 article in *Scribner's Magazine* by Dr. E. H. Van Deusen, which asserts that the poor farm woman's unrelieved isolation often gave rise to "mental pathology," a symptom of which was "distrust." Zeena, then, can be viewed not as a gratuitously evil woman but as one whose bitter reaction to her confined life was not atypical.

Mattie's position in the novel is also historically accurate. As grueling as farm life was at the time, city life for poor women was usually no better. Those who could work had to accept low wages and harsh working conditions. Mattie, a penniless orphan, was trapped.

*From *A Backward Glance* by Edith Wharton. Copyright ©1934 by Edith Wharton. Reprinted by permission of the *Estate of Edith Wharton and the Watkins/Loomis Agency.*

Sources of the Novel

Edith Wharton generally revealed little about the sources or inspiration of her fiction. She did tell us in her introduction to the 1922 edition of *Ethan Frome* and in *A Backward Glance* that she intended to write realistically about life in the New England hill country as she observed it. She also explained that she began writing the story that would become *Ethan Frome* in French while she was in Paris in 1907. She was working with a young French tutor to improve her command of the language and proposed to write for him because he was too afraid to correct her spoken French—an indication, perhaps, of just how imposing a figure the mature Edith Wharton was. The French sketch was never finished. She completed the novel, as it now stands, in Paris the following winter (1910).

Scholars have proposed that the sledding disaster in *Ethan Frome* was suggested by a sledding accident that occurred in Lenox, Massachusetts (near Wharton's summer home), in March of 1904. Four girls and a boy, juniors and seniors in high school, went coasting on a Friday afternoon. They crashed into a lamppost at the bottom of the steep Courthouse Hill in Lenox. One of the girls, Hazel Crosby, was killed, and another, Kate Spencer, suffered a facial injury that left a permanent scar. Although Edith Wharton was in Paris at the time of the accident, she became acquainted with the scarred Kate Spencer later, when they worked together at the Lenox Library. The parallels to *Ethan Frome* are obvious. Courthouse Hill, with its lamppost, corresponds to the novel's School House Hill, with its elm tree. The gash on Ethan's face recalls Kate Spencer's injury. Edith Wharton made no public mention of any connection between the incident and her novel, however, and we can only infer its influence on her.

Biographers and Wharton scholars, beginning with R.W.B. Lewis, who had access to private papers never before available, have also built a strong case to suggest that Wharton's own unhappy marriage and the painful end of her love affair with Morton Fullerton contributed to the theme of thwarted love and to the despairing tone of *Ethan Frome.*

By the time of the writing of *Ethan Frome,* Edith Wharton's marriage to Teddy had indeed become a nightmare. Unlike Ethan Frome, however, Edith Wharton abandoned the path of self-sacrifice and resignation to circumstances when she divorced her husband in 1913.

Literary Context

In *A Backward Glance,* Wharton responds to the critics who questioned her decision to write about the poor farmers of New England: "For years I had wanted to draw life as it really was in the derelict mountain villages of New England, a life even in my time, and a thousandfold more a generation earlier, utterly unlike that seen through the rose-colored spectacles of my predecessors, Mary Wilkins and Sarah Orne Jewett."* The predecessors referred to were writers whose work Wharton saw as sentimental and superficial. The New England settings she wished to convey were "grim places . . . : Mental and moral starvation were hidden away behind the paintless wooden house-fronts of the long village street, or in the isolated farmhouses on the neighboring hills."*

In *Ethan Frome,* Wharton achieved a social and psychological realism that comes closer to the bleak determinism of Theodore Dreiser's *An American Tragedy* than to the picturesque romanticism of Sarah Orne Jewett's *The Country of the Pointed Firs* (1896).

*From *A Backward Glance* by Edith Wharton. Copyright © 1934 by Edith Wharton. Reprinted by permission of the *Estate of Edith Wharton* and the *Watkins/Loomis Agency.*

Like Nathaniel Hawthorne, an earlier chronicler of the New England psyche, Wharton was preoccupied with the interplay of culture, landscape, morality, and will in the lives of her characters. In *Edith Wharton: A Biography,* R.W.B. Lewis sees Hawthorne's influence in "the sense of deepening physical chill . . . that corresponds to the inner wintriness" of Wharton's characters.

Ethan Frome is similar to the protagonist of Hawthorne's short story "Ethan Brand," a man who discovers he is guilty of the "unpardonable sin," the inability to love. His moral desolation, like that of Frome, leads him to suicide. Brand, however, succeeds in killing himself. When his incinerated remains are found, all that is left is a piece of stone in the shape of a heart. Neither Ethan Brand nor Ethan Frome is a whole man in life or death.

Wharton's choice of the name Zeena recalls the character Zenobia in Hawthorne's *The Blithedale Romance* (1852). Zenobia is a proud and commanding woman who is defeated in love and drowns herself. Zeena is a twisted heroine, a woman in whom love has turned to hate and strength into the will to destroy.

Critical Responses

The technical brilliance and verbal virtuosity of *Ethan Frome* have been recognized since its publication in 1911, although some early reviewers questioned the unrelenting pessimism of the tragic ending.

Most, however, saw the point of Ethan's tragedy and were moved by it. The reviewer for the 1912 *Bookman* felt the tragedy of *Ethan Frome* as "almost unendurably poignant, but justified by its inevitableness." He wrote:

> It is a beautiful, sad, but intensely human story, working out to its final conclusion with all the inevitability of a great Greek tragedy.

Along with repugnance for her theme, there were also questions about Wharton's choice of characters and whether or not she was fit to write about them. The reviewer for *Outlook* magazine (October 1911) seemed to think Wharton's brilliance was wasted on her subjects.

> As a piece of artistic workmanship it would be hard to overstate the quality of this story. It is conceived and executed with a unity of insight, structural skill, and feeling for style which lies only within the reach of an artist who . . . knows every resource of the art. It is to be hoped that when Mrs. Wharton writes again she will bring her great talent to bear on normal people and situations.

Others suggested that Wharton was unworthy to write about her rural characters. Such reservations persisted as late as the 1960s, when the critic Abigail Ann Hamblen wrote:

> Edith Wharton's approach to the Massachusetts "hill country" savors decidedly of the air of an aristocrat going slumming among the lower orders.
>
> —from "Edith Wharton in New England"

A few midcentury critics had trouble with the morality of *Ethan Frome*. In an incisive 1956 essay, the distinguished critic Lionel Trilling wrote of the denouement of *Ethan Frome*:

> There is . . . an image of life-in-death, of hell on earth, which is not easily forgotten: the crippled Ethan, and Zeena, his dreadful wife, and Mattie, the once charming girl he had loved, now bedridden and querulous with pain, all living out their

*From "The Morality of Inertia" from *A Gathering of Fugitives* by Lionel Trilling. Copyright ©1956 by Lionel Trilling. Reprinted by permission of *The Wylie Agency.*

death in the kitchen of the desolate Frome farm—a perpetuity of suffering memorializes a moment of passion. It is terrible to contemplate, . . . but the mind can do nothing with it, can only endure it. . . . In the context of morality, there is nothing to say about *Ethan Frome*. It presents no moral issue at all.*

—from "The Morality of Inertia"

The tide of critical opinion, however, has grown positive since the ground-breaking 1975 biography by R.W.B. Lewis and the burgeoning of feminist criticism in the 1970s and 1980s. With unprecedented access to Wharton's private journals and letters, Lewis presented a sympathetic picture of a generous, liberal-minded woman whose life was shadowed by illness, pain, and frustrated love. Feminists see Wharton as a woman who sympathized with the desire of women from all classes for a life less dependent on their social roles.

Another issue that has occupied critics since *Ethan Frome*'s publication is its frame structure and enigmatic narrator. Some early critics saw this framing device as awkward, distracting, and unnecessary. In her introduction to the 1922 edition, Wharton explains that her story about simple characters needed a complex and sophisticated narrator to act as a "sympathizing intermediary between [the] rudimentary characters and the more complicated minds" of the readers.

The contemporary critic Cynthia Griffin Wolff goes even further than Wharton and claims that the novel is really the narrator's story, not Ethan Frome's. This is made clear, Wolff argues, in Wharton's prologue when the narrator refers to the "vision" he put together from information he received and observations he made:

The novel . . . focuses on the narrator's problem: the tension between his public self and his shadow self [represented by Ethan], his terror of a seductive and enveloping void.

—from *A Feast of Words: The Triumph of Edith Wharton*

The Novel at a Glance

Ethan Frome

A **Novel Review** that includes **plot** and **setting** appears on page 49 of this study guide.

A **Literary Elements Worksheet** that focuses on **setting** and **characterization** appears on page 50 of this study guide.

Plot and Setting

The plot of *Ethan Frome* is organized around a central problem or question: How could a man like Ethan Frome become so thwarted and defeated in his aspirations for love and life? The narrative reveals the particular set of external circumstances and internal tendencies that inexorably doom Ethan, and those close to him, to a living death.

The bleak setting of the novel not only reflects its themes but also functions as one of the obstacles that Ethan must overcome if he is to fulfill his dreams. Winter lasts a long time in this isolated, nineteenth-century New England village, aptly named Starkfield, where Ethan tries to wring a living out of the poor, rocky soil and where deprivation goes beyond the lack of money.

Structure and Point of View

The novel consists of a **frame story,** presented in the prologue and in the epilogue, and an inner story, given in a **flashback,** told between the opening and closing first-person narratives. The frame functions as the story's present, in which the narrator encounters Ethan Frome at the age of fifty-two and becomes curious about this silent, lame, yet somehow striking figure.

In the flashback, which begins in Chapter I, the time is twenty-four years earlier. Ethan is twenty-eight-years old. This inner story is told from the third-person limited point of view, which de-emphasizes the narrator's responses and emphasizes Ethan's experience.

Major Characters

The Narrator of the frame story, a young engineer who works near Starkfield, pieces together a "vision" of Ethan Frome's story from various sources in the village and from his own observations when a snowstorm forces him to spend a night at the Frome farm.

Ethan Frome, in the inner story, is an inarticulate but imaginative young farmer who falls in love with a young relative of his wife's when she comes to live with the unhappy couple. In the frame story he is fifty-two and crippled, the victim of a sledding "accident" that occurred twenty-four years earlier.

Zeena (Zenobia) Frome is Ethan's wife, seven years his senior; she is bitter, domineering, and taciturn, except when obsessing on her many illnesses. Ever discontent, she grows increasingly determined to send her young relative away.

Mattie Silver, Zeena's cousin, is a penniless orphan who comes to live with the Fromes to help the "ailing" older woman. Lively yet delicate, she becomes the focus of Ethan's romantic yearnings and returns his love with loyalty and tender devotion.

Ruth Varnum (Mrs. Ned Hale), in the inner story, is Mattie's girlhood friend. She is engaged to marry Ned Hale, the local builder. Their freedom to love and marry contrasts sharply with the constraints facing Ethan and Mattie. In the frame story, Mrs. Hale is the narrator's widowed landlady and one of the people who helps him put together Ethan's story.

Themes

Ethan's story can be read as a tragic tale of **love defeated by circumstances.** Soul-crushing poverty, backbreaking work for little reward, emotional isolation, and unremitting responsibility for others seem to be Ethan Frome's inherited lot. Every attempt he makes to escape those circumstances ends in failure, culminating in his inability to find a way to either live or die with Mattie on terms of his own choosing.

Ethan's fate can also be viewed as a **tragedy of inertia** or **paralysis of will,** the inability to counter isolation, routine, silence, and ultimately death itself. Was there a way out for Ethan? Or did he submit to some dark inclination in his psyche?

Another way of looking at Ethan's tragedy is as a **failure of expression** or communication. He is crushed by the silence all around him as well as by the silence within him, which offers no creative solution to his constricted circumstances.

*A **Literary Elements Worksheet** that focuses on **theme** appears on page 51 of this study guide.*

Major Symbols

The **wintry landscape** of New England, with its snow, ice, rocky outcroppings, and freezing temperatures, reflects the emotional climate in which Ethan lives, first with his "silent" mother and then with his cold wife who speaks only to complain.

Sledding, or coasting, is associated first in the novel with the freedom, gaiety, and liveliness of youth—pleasures that the dutiful Ethan has denied himself. Then, in connection with Ned and Ruth, sledding seems to represent romance and sexual adventure. Ethan and Mattie talk of coasting in the moonlight. Ironically, their final ride becomes an embrace not of life and love but of death and defeat.

The **cat,** which is associated with Zeena, suggests the predatory side of nature, a natural enemy to birds and mice, which are associ-

*A **Literary Elements Worksheet** that focuses on **symbols** appears on page 52 of this study guide.*

ated with Mattie's weak and delicate nature. The cat also has a sinister, almost supernatural quality, a haunting presence that never allows Ethan to forget his ties to Zeena. It is the cat that precipitates the breaking of the pickle dish and brings an end to Ethan and Mattie's peaceful interlude. Even in her absence, Zeena has triumphed.

Tone

The tone of the novel is bitterly and unrelentingly ironic. Nothing turns out as Ethan hopes or expects, although the reader, knowing his fate from the start, is allowed no such illusions. For example, his dreams of becoming an engineer are cut off by family troubles. Zeena, whose voice in the house he initially welcomes, turns silent. The intimacy he has with Mattie, which he hopes will go on forever, comes to an abrupt end, and most striking of all, the wished-for quick death becomes an agonizingly long life.

Introducing the Novel

Options

DISCUSSION AND ROLE-PLAY

Putting Yourself in Their Place

Ask students to gather in small groups and discuss what they imagine it would be like to live on a small, isolated farm during a long, freezing winter. Remind them that they would have no modern conveniences, such as radio, television, telephone, computer, car, central heating, or public transportation. How do they imagine they would feel in such circumstances? What problems would they have to solve? Then, have them try to imagine a husband and wife, with money only for the bare necessities, living on such a farm in nineteenth-century New England. How do they think the couple's circumstances might affect their relationship? Students may want to role-play the farmer and his wife, discussing their experience of the long, cold winter on the farm.

HISTORICAL RESEARCH

Farm or Factory?

Suggest that students work with partners to gather factual information about the lives of poor women in New England in the late nineteenth century. One partner can concentrate on the economic and social conditions facing farm women and the other on the lives of women working in shops, factories, or domestic service. Here are some questions students can use to focus their research:

- What economic and social options were open to young women from poor families in nineteenth-century New England?
- How was marital status likely to affect such a woman's position?
- What rights and responsibilities did marriage offer a woman of that time?
- How might women have responded, both physically and mentally, to the options open to them?

Students can share their findings by summarizing for the class how the opportunities of these nineteenth-century women compare and contrast with those of working-class women today.

INFERRING/PREDICTING

Film Clip

Review the film version of *Ethan Frome* (available from Buena Vista Films, 1992), and choose a segment featuring the young Ethan in his wintry New England setting. After showing the segment to the class, open a discussion with the following questions:

- What is your first impression of Ethan Frome?
- What is your first impression of the setting in which he lives?
- How might Ethan respond to the conditions of his life?
- Does this glimpse of the setting and the title character lead you to expect a tragedy or a comedy?

SPEAKING AND LISTENING

Star-crossed Lovers

Tell students that one of the major themes of *Ethan Frome* is thwarted, or frustrated, love. Ask them to think of other novels, stories, plays, or films about couples who do *not* live happily ever after. Ask students to write down the names of those characters and the works in which they appear (Shakespeare's *Romeo and Juliet,* for example) and post the names prominently in the classroom. Then, have students discuss what keeps those fictional couples apart, and have them compile a list of the obstacles they name. As they read *Ethan Frome,* they can check off any similar obstacles that Ethan and Mattie face.

Plot Synopsis and Literary Elements

Prologue–Chapter II

Plot Synopsis

The novel opens with a prologue, in which the first-person narrator directly states that he has been piecing together the story of a lame man named Ethan Frome whom he sees daily at the post office. The narrator, an engineer working on the construction of a power plant in rural New England, is forced, due to labor unrest, to spend the winter in nearby Starkfield, an isolated village in the Berkshire Mountains of western Massachusetts. Struck not only by Ethan's hobbled gait and the great red gash on his forehead but also by his "bleak and unapproachable" demeanor, the narrator learns from a local man, Harmon Gow, and from his landlady, Mrs. Ned Hale, that Ethan Frome and a companion were in a terrible "smashup" on a sled twenty-four years earlier. Sensing a defeat in Ethan that transcends poverty or physical suffering, the narrator wishes to fill in the gaps in this account of him. He gets an opportunity to do so when he engages Ethan to drive him to and from the train to work each day. One night while the pair are returning to Starkfield, they get caught in a snowstorm that so exhausts the horse and the men that Ethan is forced to stop at his own farmhouse and offer the narrator a night's shelter. Together the two enter the hallway of a dimly lighted farmhouse and are greeted by the sound of a droning female voice from within. The narrator reveals that it was what he saw that night at the farmhouse that shaped his vision of Ethan's story.

A long series of ellipses ends the prologue, and the time of the action and the point of view shift dramatically in Chapter I. We meet Ethan as a much younger man, and his story is told in the third person. Forced to give up his studies at a technological college when his father dies, Ethan labors to eke out a meager living from his poor farm and antiquated sawmill. His "sickly" wife, Zeena, has arranged for her young cousin, Mattie Silver, to live in and help her with the housework. In the year that Mattie has lived with the Fromes, she has not proved much help to Zeena but has become the one joy in Ethan's bleak life. On a cold winter night, Ethan walks through dark, silent Starkfield toward the lighted church where Mattie Silver is enjoying herself at a dance. Ethan shivers with jealousy and dread when he sees her savoring the attentions of lively Denis Eady, the grocer's son, and when he recalls how his wife has spoken ominously of Mattie's marrying Denis and leaving the farm.

Feeling shy, Ethan waits in the shadows as the dancers leave the church and is alarmed when Denis confidently offers to drive Mattie home in his father's new sleigh. Feeling that she might accept, Ethan waits silently in an agony of suspense and is elated when she rejects the offer. Ethan quickly catches up with her, links his arm in hers, and enjoys, for a time, the security of knowing that Mattie prefers his company. They walk past School House Hill, where young couples go sledding, and Ethan promises to take Mattie out one moonlit night and steer her safely around the big elm tree that lies at the foot of the steep incline. As they head toward home, darker thoughts trouble Ethan, and he seeks reassurance that Mattie will not leave the farm. Mattie senses that Zeena is displeased with her, and when the pair reach the farmhouse, the key is not in its usual place, under the mat. As they fumble in search of it, Zeena appears in the doorway with a lantern, a witchlike specter, putting a quick end to Ethan's fantasies of a warm and secure future with Mattie.

Literary Elements

Structure and Setting: There is a gap of twenty-four years between the time of the **frame story** and that of the **inner story,** which begins in Chapter I. The events of the inner story take place in the winter of Ethan Frome's twenty-eighth year. His wife's cousin Mattie has been living with the couple for about a year. The frame story also takes place in winter, and this structure and setting seem to imprison Ethan in a perpetual winter, where all promises of spring prove illusory or transient.

Characterization: In the prologue the narrator **directly characterizes** Ethan Frome, but his descriptions are strangely contradictory. He calls Ethan "the most striking figure in Starkfield, though he was but the ruin of a man." He speaks also of his "careless powerful look . . . in spite of a lameness checking each step." In appearance he is "grizzled" and "grave," and "his taciturnity was respected." In an instance of **indirect characterization,** Harmon Gow, a villager, conjectures that though the Fromes are tough, Ethan may have been defeated by "too many winters" in Starkfield.

Plot: Chapter I reveals the central **external conflicts:** Ethan against the chilling burdens of cold, poverty, and silence and the antagonism of his wife, Zeena, toward the one joy in his life, Mattie Silver.

The **exposition** continues in Chapter II, with the introduction of an important **internal conflict.** Ethan's love for Mattie fills him with romantic yearnings, but he cannot express those feelings, just as he is unable to find a way to actualize any of his dreams.

Foreshadowing: In Chapter II, as Ethan and Mattie walk home arm in arm from the church dance, they pass the hill where the young people of the town go sledding. Mattie talks excitedly about how the young lovers Ned and Ruth nearly crashed into the elm at the bottom of the hill, ironically foreshadowing the "smashup" that looms in their future.

Chapters III–IV

Plot Synopsis

The next morning while Ethan is chopping wood, he reflects on his distaste for the wheezing body of his ever-ailing wife and his desire to kiss Mattie, the once-pale young girl who has come to life in his home after having been orphaned and left penniless by a dishonest father. With a vague dread fueled by Zeena's ominous silence the night before, Ethan returns home in the middle of the day. To his surprise he finds Zeena outfitted for travel and determined to seek treatment from a new doctor in one of the larger towns in the region. Ethan immediately calculates that her journey will require a night away from home, leaving him alone overnight with Mattie for the first time. He tries to behave normally but cannot bring himself to take the long drive into town with his wife. As an excuse for not driving her, he claims he has to collect some money from Andrew Hale, the builder who buys his lumber. Absorbed in her pains and patent medicines, Zeena seems unaware of Ethan's state of mind and allows herself to be driven to town by the hired man, Jotham Powell.

As soon as Zeena leaves, Ethan hurries to town to deliver his lumber so he can return home quickly for supper with Mattie. Worried about Zeena's habit of overspending while away from home, Ethan tries but fails to get a loan from Andrew Hale. On the way home he imagines the pleasure of sharing a meal with Mattie in the warm kitchen. The prospect rouses him to remember how much he enjoyed human company before his father's accident and his mother's long, silent illness accustomed him to his lonely existence on the farm. He remembers that when Zeena, a relative of his mother's, first came to nurse the old woman, he welcomed her voice in the house and the efficient way she managed the sickroom. Faced with a return to that awful solitude when his mother died, Ethan fatefully asked Zeena to marry him. Soon after, he discovered that he could not sell the farm and pursue his dream of becoming an engineer. Zeena, too, seemed to abandon whatever hopes she had for the marriage, and silence once again descended on the farm, until Mattie arrived.

Today, however, Ethan has hope: Mattie is at home waiting for him. Not even the fear that Denis Eady might be heading out to see Mattie can completely quell his happy anticipation, and when Mattie answers the door wearing a crimson ribbon in her hair, Ethan is enchanted. Shyly but happily they sit down to a brightly set table, until the cat accidentally breaks a dish that Zeena prizes, and thoughts of Zeena come between them. Their good spirits return, however, when Ethan reassures Mattie that he can glue the pieces together and replace the dish before Zeena discovers the damage.

Literary Elements

Plot: Tensions rise in the **conflict** between Ethan and Zeena over Mattie's continued presence in the household. They are unexpectedly eased when a seemingly preoccupied Zeena announces that she is making an overnight journey to consult a new doctor.
Complications develop, however, when the cat breaks a prized dish of Zeena's that Mattie uses to decorate the table she sets for her and Ethan.

Imagery: Lack of color, light, and warmth in the landscape and in human beings is used to suggest a lack of vitality and love. Ethan looks at Zeena in "the pale light reflected from the banks of snow . . . her face . . . drawn and bloodless." Mattie, on the other hand, is at home in the warm, bright kitchen where the sun slants "through the south window." Zeena is a wintry figure, whereas the geraniums from Mattie's summer garden brighten the house as Mattie does.

Characterization: Both Mattie and Zeena are characterized by the contrasting accounts of their early days at the Frome farm. Zeena came to help with a dying woman and was efficient and useful while she was needed. Later Mattie also came to help a sick woman (Zeena), but she arrived in a weakened state herself and was of little help. Mattie, however, grows healthier and happier over time, while Zeena grows ever more discontent and self-absorbed.

Symbolism: During the evening that Ethan and Mattie are alone together, they are seldom free of reminders of Zeena. The cat, in particular, seems to represent Zeena's persistent intrusion or spectral presence. The animal constantly interposes itself between the couple and seems to claim Zeena's rocker as its own. Finally, it effectively disturbs the couple's harmony by breaking a treasured dish of Zeena's that Mattie dares to use.

Chapters V–VI

Plot Synopsis

After supper, Ethan and Mattie sit in the kitchen, Ethan smoking near the stove and Mattie sewing in the lamplight. At first, Ethan enjoys the peaceful intimacy of the scene and allows himself to believe they will have many such evenings. He even talks of how they might have gone sledding and how he would steer Mattie carefully around the dangerous elm tree. However, when he urges Mattie to sit near him in Zeena's rocker, they are both reminded of the absent woman, and their chatter becomes constrained. Longing for some physical intimacy but at a loss to achieve it, Ethan alludes to seeing a young engaged couple kissing. When Mattie blushes deeply, Ethan becomes even more awkward, talking about her being the next to get married. Alarmed, Mattie immediately starts worrying that Zeena wants to get rid of her, and both resolve, with little success, to try not to think about Zeena. Sitting there with a mere length of material between them, saying little but feeling much, they both seem forever bound and forever separated. Finally Ethan leans over and kisses the end of her needlework. Mattie gently pulls the material to her and rises to leave the room. Ethan watches her depart, thinking that "he had not even touched her hand."

At breakfast the next morning, Ethan is "irrationally happy" just to have experienced what life with Mattie would be like. He plans the day carefully in order to have a little more time alone with her and to repair the broken dish before Zeena is brought home by Jotham Powell. However, icy weather and an injury to one of the horses delays his plan to haul some lumber into town. By the time he gets to Eady's store to buy glue, he is already very late, but he pushes on home as fast as possible, hoping that Jotham has been similarly delayed. When he arrives, Mattie whispers to him that Zeena has come home and gone up to her room without a word. Mattie goes about her work carefully, just as she had the night before, but with Zeena home the ominous silence of the household, along with Ethan's anxiety, has returned.

Literary Elements

Theme and Symbolism: Although Ethan is deeply excited to be alone with Mattie, he says or does very little to express his feelings directly. His words are few and highly mundane; they do not come close to expressing his inner feelings. Their talk of sledding is a **symbolic expression** of their unstated desire for romance and adventure. When the evening is over, Ethan regrets that he did not even touch Mattie's hand, managing only to caress the edge of the material she was sewing.

Plot and Theme: Unforeseen **complications,** such as icy weather and an injured horse, prevent Ethan from getting back from town before Zeena's return. Such mundane obstacles are concrete reminders of the huge social, economic, and psychological barriers that stand in the way of Ethan and Mattie's love.

Characterization and Imagery: Wharton frequently uses images of spring and summer to express what Mattie means to Ethan. For him she is the soft side of nature, the opposite of the wintry landscape he normally inhabits. Her face is "like a wheat-field under a summer breeze." Her voice seems "a rustling covert leading to enchanted glades." Her hands while sewing move "just as . . . a pair of birds make short perpendicular flights over a nest."

Chapters VII–VIII

Plot Synopsis

When Ethan goes up to Zeena's room to get her for supper, she tells him that she is suffering from "complications" and that the new doctor has said she needs a hired girl so that she may rest completely. When Ethan protests that he cannot afford the wages, she alludes to the money he intended to get from Andrew Hale and announces that the girl has already been hired and will arrive the next day. The news angers Ethan, and the two argue openly for the first time in their miserable seven years together. Ethan tries to overcome Zeena's determination, but he is finally cornered when she announces that she intends to save him money by sending Mattie away. Overwhelmed now by his powerlessness, he goes to the kitchen and spills out his despair to Mattie, kiss-ing her heedlessly and crying out prophetically, "You can't go Matt! I won't let you!"

Knowing that Zeena will never change her mind, Mattie, although despondent, tries to act bravely for Ethan's sake, but both know that a delicate and penniless girl like Mattie will soon be ground down by the harsh conditions she will face in domestic service or in the factories.

Then Zeena unexpectedly appears in the kitchen, with a renewed appetite and a rare affability, buoyed perhaps by the knowledge that she has found a way to deprive Ethan and Mattie of any pleasure they may have found with each other. Her mood changes abruptly, however, when she discovers the fragments of the broken dish while searching for one of her medicines. Ethan tries to deflect blame by claiming the cat broke it, but Zeena is not assuaged. When Mattie admits to having used the dish to brighten the supper table the night before, Zeena, in a fury of resentment and perhaps jealousy, accuses Mattie of destroying the one thing she most treasured.

Spending the night in a little unheated "study" he has made for himself in the back of the parlor, Ethan is warmed by a note left for him by Mattie: "Don't trouble, Ethan." He rages inwardly against the prospect of wasting his life with a bitter woman who will never be happy with their circumstances. He dreams of escaping out west with Mattie and begins to write Zeena a letter explaining that he is leaving her with the assets of the farm and mill. Then he realizes that the farm is mortgaged, and he doesn't even have the money to buy the train tickets west. He is trapped by his poverty and knows himself to be "a prisoner for life." He remembers that this was the night he and Mattie talked of going sledding in the moonlight.

In the kitchen the next morning, Ethan is cheered by the sight of Mattie going about her chores, and he begins to hope that Zeena will change her mind. When he learns that Zeena has made arrangements for the hired hand to transport Mattie and her trunk that very day, Ethan realizes that he must take quick and dramatic measures if he is to prevent his separation from Mattie. In a state of confused desperation, he rushes off to town to ask Andrew Hale for a loan. This time he is willing to swallow his pride and emphasize Zeena's pressing need for hired help. On the way he meets Mrs. Hale, who expresses genuine sympathy for Ethan's personal sacrifice. This unusual recognition of his circumstances fills Ethan with shame. He cannot bring himself to take advantage of these good people's sympathy for him, and he turns and walks back slowly to the farm.

Literary Elements

Plot and Theme: The **conflict** between Ethan and Zeena comes to a head in Chapter VII when Ethan realizes that Zeena is determined to send Mattie away. Although he opposes her plan, Zeena is the more determined of the two. In contrast to Ethan's **weakness of will,** or dreamy ineffectiveness, Zeena has a plan and has taken concrete steps to get what she wants.

Symbolism: The intensity of Zeena's emotion when she discovers the broken dish reveals its powerful **symbolic** dimensions. In a rage of anger and resentment, she accuses Mattie of taking from her "the one I cared for most of all," suggesting at once her jealousy of Mattie and the depths of her material and emotional deprivation. In the last line of Chapter VII, Zeena is described as leaving the room with the "bits of broken glass . . . as if she carried a dead body," the lifeless remains of her relationship with Ethan and of any hopes for love or beauty in her drab life.

Theme and Irony: As a last attempt at a practical solution, Ethan plans to ask Andrew Hale for a loan. If he and Mattie can escape New England and go west, perhaps they can live and love freely. However, when he encounters a rare expression of sympathy from Mrs. Hale, he cannot make use of the Hale's goodwill to free himself. Instead, he sees it as a reason to return to his life of self-sacrifice.

Chapter IX–Epilogue

Plot Synopsis

After dinner, Ethan defies Zeena and insists that he, not the hired hand, will drive Mattie to the train. He and Mattie go off in the sleigh, but Ethan, wanting to stretch out the little time they have left together, takes a detour to Shadow Pond. They recall the happy time they spent together there last summer at a church picnic. As the sun begins to set, they return to the Starkfield road and talk disconsolately of what

Mattie might do on her own to support herself. Ethan apologizes for his inability to help her, and she lets him know that she understands his situation, having found the letter he had begun to write to Zeena. Filled with despair, they profess their love for each other, and Ethan says that he would almost rather see her dead than married to someone else. Approaching School House Hill just as darkness falls, they remember their plan to go coasting, and Ethan suggests they do it now. They find a sled among the spruces and coast down the hill, with Ethan expertly steering around the big elm at the bottom. Exhilarated, they climb back up the hill and embrace, unable to part. Suddenly Mattie says that she wants Ethan to take her down the hill again, this time without missing the elm tree—so they will "never come up anymore." Ethan is astounded, but the thought of returning to life alone with Zeena is unbearable. He takes the front seat and lets the sled rush straight for the elm. With Mattie clinging to him in a mutual pact of death, the sled hits the tree.

In a few moments, Ethan becomes aware of the sky and of a twittering noise near him, like that of a wounded animal. Mattie is alive beside him, injured and calling his name. They have failed to "fetch" the death they sought.

In the epilogue the narrator resumes his account of entering Ethan Frome's farmhouse and hearing the "querulous drone" of a female voice. Twenty-four years have passed. In the kitchen are two worn and poorly clad women—one short and dark eyed, huddled immobile by the fire; the other tall and thin, moving about the shabby room. It is the seated one whose voice he had heard complaining when he entered. Ethan introduces the mobile one as his wife and the seated one as "Miss Mattie Silver."

The next day the narrator returns to his landlady, Mrs. Hale, the former Ruth Varnum, who was Mattie's good friend when both were young. Mrs. Hale confides that she cared for Mattie after the crash. Zeena eventually brought Mattie, now permanently disabled, back to the farm. The three have

remained together on the farm ever since, their poverty and isolation nearly complete. Mrs. Hale reports that Mattie soured as a result of her suffering but that Zeena seemed to find renewed strength in her role as nurse and caretaker. In Mrs. Hale's opinion it is Ethan who has suffered the most. She reveals that in her opinion it would have been better if Mattie had died the night of the crash so that Ethan might have lived.

Literary Elements

Plot and Theme: As Mattie's departure approaches, Ethan is defeated by Zeena, by hostile circumstances, and perhaps by his own lack of will, imagination, or power of expression. The only question that remains is whether he and Mattie will submit to their seemingly inevitable separation. Tension mounts when Ethan insists on driving Mattie to the station, and the **climax** occurs when they stop to take a last coast down School House Hill.

Symbolism: Ethan and Mattie's climatic **coast down School House Hill** has been foreshadowed throughout the novel. Both repeatedly refer to it as an exciting prospect, but they also put the ride off until the moment they are forced to part. Their first ride down seems to demonstrate Ethan's control; ironically, he is helpless to steer them around their social and economic obstacles. Their final ride is meant to be an escape from their circumstances. In the end they see death as the only resolution of an intolerable situation.

Irony: The central irony of the novel is that Mattie and Ethan fail to achieve even the terrible release of death. Instead, they awake to a long life of pain and joyless proximity. With an even more bitter irony the now disabled Mattie has taken on Zeena's traits, and she is the one with the "querulous drone" that the narrator hears. Zeena, on the other hand, seems to have reverted to her caretaker role, and Ethan now has Mattie with him "forever" in a terrible inversion of his earlier romantic fantasies.

Reader's Log: Model

Reading actively

In your reader's log you record your ideas, questions, comments, interpretations, guesses, predictions, reflections, challenges—any responses you have to the books you are reading.

Keep your reader's log with you while you are reading. You can stop at any time to write. You may want to pause several times during your reading time to capture your thoughts while they are fresh in your mind, or you may want to read without interruption and write when you come to a stopping point such as the end of a chapter or the end of the book.

Each entry you make in your reader's log should include the date, the title of the book you are reading, and the pages you have read since your last entry (pages ____ to ____).

Example

Sept. 21

<u>Fahrenheit 451</u>

pages 3 to 68

This book reminds me a lot of another book we read in class last year, <u>1984</u> by George Orwell. They're both books about the future—<u>1984</u> was written in the 1940s so it was the future then—a bad future where the government is very repressive and you can be arrested for what you think, say, or read. They're also both about a man and a woman who try to go against the system together. <u>Fahrenheit 451</u> is supposed to be about book censorship, but I don't think it's just about that—I think it's also about people losing their brain power by watching TV all the time and not thinking for themselves. <u>1984</u> did not have a very happy ending, and I have a feeling this book isn't going to either.

Exchanging ideas

Exchange reader's logs with a classmate and respond in writing to each other's most recent entries. (Your entries can be about the same book or different ones.) You might ask a question, make a comment, give your own opinion, recommend another book— in other words, discuss anything that's relevant to what you are reading.

Or: Ask your teacher, a family member, or a friend to read your most recent entries and write a reply to you in your reader's log.

Or: With your teacher's guidance, find an online pen pal in another town, state, or country and have a continuing book dialogue by e-mail.

Reader's Log: Starters

When I started reading this book, I thought . . .

I changed my mind about . . . because . . .

My favorite part of the book was . . .

My favorite character was . . . because . . .

I was surprised when . . .

I predict that . . .

I liked the way the writer . . .

I didn't like . . . because . . .

This book reminded me of . . .

I would (wouldn't) recommend this book to a friend because . . .

This book made me feel . . .

This book made me think . . .

This book made me realize . . .

While I was reading I pictured . . . (Draw or write your response.)

The most important thing about this book is . . .

If I were (name of character), I would (wouldn't) have . . .

What happened in this book was very realistic (unrealistic) because . . .

My least favorite character was . . . because . . .

I admire (name of character) for . . .

One thing I've noticed about the author's style is . . .

If I could be any character in this book, I would be . . . because . . .

I agree (disagree) with the writer about . . .

I think the title is a good (strange/misleading) choice because . . .

A better title for this book would be . . . because . . .

In my opinion, the most important word (sentence/paragraph) in this book is . . . because . . .

(Name of character) reminds me of myself because . . .

(Name of character) reminds me of somebody I know because . . .

If I could talk to (name of character), I would say . . .

When I finished this book, I still wondered . . .

This book was similar to (different from) other books I've read because it . . .

This book was similar to (different from) other books by this writer because it . . .

I think the main thing the writer was trying to say was . . .

This book was better (worse) than the movie version because . . .

(Event in book) reminded me of (something that happened to me) when . . .

Responding to the text Draw a line down the middle of a page in your reader's log. On the left side, copy a meaningful passage from the book you're reading—perhaps a bit of dialogue, a description, or a character's thought. (Be sure to note the number of the page you copied it from—you or somebody else may want to find it later.) On the right side, write your response to the quotation. Why did you choose it? Did it puzzle you? confuse you? strike a chord? What does it mean to you?

Example

Quotation	Response
"It is a truth universally acknowledged, that a single man in possession of a good fortune must be in want of a wife." (page 1)	This is the first sentence of the book. When I first read it I thought the writer was serious—it seemed like something people might have believed when it was written. Soon I realized she was making fun of that attitude. I saw the movie <u>Pride and Prejudice</u>, but it didn't have a lot of funny parts, so I didn't expect the book to be funny at all. It is though, but not in an obvious way.

Creating a dialogue journal Draw a line down the middle of a page in your reader's log. On the left side, comment on the book you're reading—the plot so far, your opinion of the characters, or specifics about the style in which the book is written. On the right side of the page, your teacher or a classmate will provide a response to your comments. Together you create an ongoing dialogue about the novel as you are reading it.

Example

Your Comment	Response
The Bennet girls really seem incredibly silly. They seem to care only about getting married to someone rich or going to balls. That is all their parents discuss, too. The one who isn't like that, Mary, isn't realistic either, though. And why doesn't anyone work?!	I wasn't really bothered by their discussion of marriage and balls. I expected it because I saw the movie <u>Emma</u>, and it was like this, too. What I don't understand is why the parents call each other "Mr." and "Mrs."—everything is so formal. I don't think women of that class were supposed to work back then. And people never <u>really</u> work on TV shows or in the movies or in other books, do they?

Name _____ Date _____

Group Discussion Log

Group members

_____

_____

_____

_____

_____

Book discussed

Title: _____

Author: _____

Pages ____ to ____

Three interesting things said by members of the group

_____

_____

_____

_____

_____

_____

_____

What we did well today as a group

_____

_____

_____

_____

What we could improve

_____

_____

_____

_____

Our next discussion will be on _____. We will discuss pages _____ to _____.

Glossary and Vocabulary

- **Vocabulary Words** are preceded by an asterisk (*) and appear in the Vocabulary Worksheets.
- Words are listed in their order of appearance.
- The definition and the part of speech are based on the way the word is used in the chapter. For other uses of the word, check a dictionary.

Prologue and Chapter I

*punctually *adv.:* in a timely manner.

*mien *n.:* air; bearing.

*taciturnity *n.:* habit of silence; disinclination to talk.

*degenerate *adj.:* falling below a former standard; degraded.

*chafed *v.:* uncomfortable or irritated.

*retarding *v.:* slowing; holding back.

*colloquially *adj.:* informally; conversationally.

horse-hair *n.:* fabric made from the manes and tails of horses, used to cover and stuff furniture.

mahogany *n.:* fine-grained reddish hardwood used to make fine furniture.

Carcel lamp *n.:* lamp that steadily pumps oil up its wick, causing a gurgling sound; invented by the Frenchman B. G. Carcel (1750–1812).

*innocuous *adj.:* harmless.

*reticent *adj.:* silent; unwilling to speak.

*initiation *n.:* knowledge not widely shared.

water-mills *n.:* old-fashioned machines that use water power to saw logs.

*sentient *adj.:* capable of feeling and perceiving.

*allusion *n.:* indirect reference.

*conditional *n.:* state of uncertainty or doubt.

exanimate *adj.:* lifeless; dead.

*wraith *n.:* ghost; apparition.

Dipper *n.:* constellation of stars.

Orion *n.:* constellation of stars.

peristyle *n.:* short, decorative columns at the base of a New England–style church steeple.

*declivity *n.:* downward slope.

harmonium *n.:* type of reed organ.

fascinator *n.:* woman's head scarf.

*suppleness *n.:* easily adaptable.

*effrontery *n.:* brashness; boldness.

*demurred *v.:* objected; protested.

*fatuity *n.:* foolishness; naiveté.

*latent *adj.:* presently inactive or hidden.

*incisively *adv.:* sharply.

Chapter II

*obscurity *n.:* darkness.

*loutish *adj.:* clumsy; unrefined.

cutter *n.:* small one-horse sleigh.

*incredulous *adj.:* unbelieving.

*eluded *v.:* got away from; avoided.

rills *n.:* small brooks or streams.

*disdainfully *adv.:* with an air of superiority.

*balm *n.:* soothing ointment.

*reverberated *v.:* echoed.

*suffused *v.:* spread over; filled.

*conspire *v.:* plot, scheme.

*tremulous *adj.:* quivering; trembling.

counterpane *n.:* bedspread.

crimping-pins *n.:* curlers.

*precision *n.:* exactness; sharpness.

*repugnant *adj.:* hateful; strongly distasteful.

Chapter III

*scintillating *adj.:* sparkling; brilliant.

*perceptible *adj.:* visible; discernible.

indentured *v.:* forced to work without pay.

*induced *v.:* persuaded.

*tangible *adj.:* concrete; solid.

*obstinate *adj.:* stubborn.

bandbox *n.:* lightweight cylindrical box for carrying clothing.

*sedentary *adj.:* having to do with sitting; inactive.

*querulous *adj.:* having to do with complaints and complaining.

*imprudence *n.:* lack of caution or wisdom.

Chapter IV

*extinguished *v.:* destroyed.

*inarticulate *adj.:* unable to express oneself in words.

*convivial *adj.:* sociable; cheerful.

*volubility *n.:* talkativeness.

*pathological *adj.:* pertaining to sickness or illness.

*inevitable *adj.:* certain; incapable of being avoided.

*supposition *n.:* possible explanation; guess.

*opulence *n.:* wealth.

*genially *adv.:* pleasantly.

*lustrous *adj.:* bright; glowing.

*insatiable *adj.:* incapable of being satisfied.

*implored *v.:* begged.

*disconsolately *adv.:* cheerlessly; in a downcast manner.

Chapter V

*indolent *adj.:* relaxed; lazy.

*countenance *n.:* face.

*superseded *adj.:* replaced.

*obliterated *v.:* wiped out any trace of.

*constraint *n.:* restriction; reserve.

*luxuriated *v.:* indulged pleasurably.

wainscot *n.:* woodwork at the base of an interior wall.

*spectral *adj.:* ghostlike.

*arrest *v.:* halt; stop.

*languidly *adv.:* listlessly; wearily.

Chapter VI

traveller's joy *n.:* flowering vine.

*self-derision *n.:* ridiculing oneself.

*solace *n.:* comfort; consolation.

*aver *v.:* declare; assert.

*ponderous *adj.:* slow moving.

*perfunctory *adj.:* performed without interest or enthusiasm.

*ominous *adj.:* threatening; foreboding.

*stolid *adj.:* stubborn; fixed.

Chapter VII

*rigidity *n.:* stiffness.

*felicitous *adj.:* happy sounding; pleasant.

*prestige *n.:* importance; status.

*resolute *adj.:* determined; firm.

*transfixed *adj.:* motionless.

*wrath *n.:* anger.

*recrimination *n.:* charge and countercharge.

almshouse *n.:* institution where the poor are housed; poorhouse.

*imminent *adj.:* immediate.

*inexorable *adj.:* unalterable; relentless.

*vehemence *n.:* intensity.

*antipathy *n.:* hatred.

*compunction *n.:* sorrow; regret.

*animosity *n.:* ill will; hostility.

*affability *n.:* friendliness; goodwill.

Chapter VIII

*protuberances *n.:* things that stick or thrust outward.

*incessant *adj.:* never ending; ceaseless.

*injunction *n.:* command; order.

huckabuck towel *n.:* towel of strong, absorbent fabric.

*ebullition *n.:* boiling up; outburst.

*benevolence *n.:* kindness; goodwill.

lumbago *n.:* painful rheumatism of the lumbar region.

plasters *n.:* dressings consisting of a film of cloth spread with a medicated substance.

*repining *n.:* complaining; expressing discontent.

*destitute *adj.:* suffering extreme want; poverty-stricken.

Chapter IX–Epilogue

*monotonous *adj.:* repetitive; unchanging.

boles *n.:* tree trunks.

*aromatic *adj.:* fragrant; sweet smelling.

*facetious *adj.:* wise cracking; joking.

*devious *adj.:* winding; twisting.

*adjured *v.:* commanded; entreated.

*discursively *adv.:* passing idly from one topic to another.

*erratic *adj.:* wayward; unpredictable.

*feint *n.:* pretense.

*audacity *n.:* boldness; bravery.

*exultantly *adv.:* with great excitement and joy.

*avowal *n.:* open declaration.

*abhorrent *adj.:* hateful.

*sombre (also spelled *somber*) *adj.:* grave; solemn.

*lineaments *n.:* outlines.

Sirius *n.:* the Dog Star, which is the brightest fixed star.

*excruciating *adj.:* agonizing.

*slatternly *adj.:* untidy; unkempt.

*opaque *adj.:* blank; dull; unintelligible.

*austere *adj.:* simple; unadorned.

*tentatively *adv.:* uncertainly.

*conjectures *n.:* guesses; surmises.

*evoked *v.:* called forth; brought out.

First Thoughts

1. If you saw a man like Ethan Frome in a public place, would you be as curious about him as the narrator is about Ethan Frome? How would such a man appear to you?

Shaping Interpretations

2. What details of Ethan's appearance and manner does the narrator provide as he observes him in the post office? How would you sum up the narrator's attitude toward him?

3. What conclusions does the narrator draw about Ethan's choices and **character**?

4. Winter functions both as the **setting** and as a recurring **symbol** in the novel. What is the first mention of winter in the prologue? With whom is it associated and with what symbolic overtones?

5. How does Mrs. Hale respond when asked about Ethan Frome? How does her reaction mirror Ethan's demeanor?

6. The narrator describes his entry into the Frome farmhouse in **images** of light and dark. What are some of these images, and what relationship between light and dark do they suggest? What other sensory experience makes a striking impression on the narrator?

7. In the **inner story** we first see a younger Ethan and Mattie together. How might Mattie feel about Ethan? What details in the text lead you to draw this conclusion?

8. What do you think is Zeena's **motivation** for talking to Ethan about Mattie marrying Denis Eady?

Connecting with the Text

9. On the basis of the first two chapters, do you feel any sympathy for Zeena? As you continue to read, monitor your feelings toward her based on your growing understanding of her situation and character.

Extending the Text

10. Do you think Ethan's alternating feelings of joy and fear are typical of a young man in love, or are they responses unique to his situation or character? What circumstances presented in the novel help to explain his ups and downs?

READING CHECK

a. Where does the narrator first see Ethan Frome?

b. How does the narrator begin to put together Ethan Frome's story?

c. What does he find out happened to Ethan twenty-four years earlier?

d. In the inner story, why has Mattie Silver come to the Frome farm?

e. What interest does Ethan share with Mattie?

f. What does Zeena say to frighten Ethan?

Writing Opportunity

Develop your opinion into a paragraph. Update your opinion as you continue the novel.

Reading Strategies: Prologue–Chapter II

Ethan Frome

Understanding Characterization

There is a twenty-four-year time span between the opening of the frame story (in the prologue) and the beginning of the inner story (in Chapters I and II). How does the **characterization** of twenty-eight-year-old Ethan in Chapters I and II contrast with that of the fifty-two-year-old Ethan presented in the prologue?

In the circle on the left, list descriptions of Ethan's character at fifty-two that contrast with the way he is portrayed at twenty-eight. In the right-hand circle, list characteristics that distinguish Ethan at twenty-eight. In the overlapping circle in the center, list the traits in Ethan's character that remain the same over the years.

Ethan at Twenty-eight   Ethan at Fifty-two

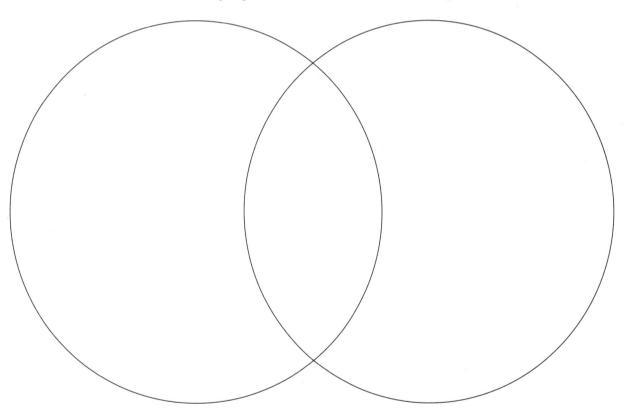

FOLLOW-UP: Use the material in the diagram to write a paragraph, summarizing how much or how little Ethan has changed in twenty-four years.

The Accident

The sledding disaster that lamed Ethan Frome may have been suggested by this account of a true event.

"Fatal Coasting Accident"

. . . Miss Hazel Crosby, a junior in the Lenox high school, was fatally and several companions seriously injured in a coasting accident in Lenox yesterday afternoon soon after four o'clock.

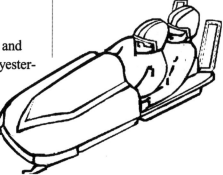

The young people were on a "double ripper" coasting sled, sweeping down a very steep hill at a tremendous rate of speed, when the fatality occurred. At the foot of the hill the sled veered and crashed into a lamppost, fatally injuring Miss Crosby and fracturing the limbs of three others.

THE DEAD.

Miss Hazel Crosby, right leg fractured in three places, left leg in one place, lower jaw broken, internal injuries.

THE INJURED.

Miss Crissey Henry, serious concussion of the brain, bad injury to side of face, injured internally.

Miss Lucy Brown, thigh fractured between knee and hip, cut on face under chin, cut in back of head.

Miss Kate Spencer, dislocation of right hip joint.

Mansuit Schmitt, contusions of head and body.

Miss Crosby was taken to the House of Mercy in this city last evening where she died at 11:30 o'clock. The fractures were reduced and everything possible was done for her, but the efforts of the skilled surgeons and doctors were without avail.

Miss Henry was taken to her home, and her condition was such that for a time her recovery was despaired of. Of those who survived the accident, she is the most seriously injured, but will recover.

SCENE OF ACCIDENT.

The scene of the accident is out a short distance from the Curtis hotel, in the center of Lenox. . . .

Court House hill as it is called is exceedingly steep and for some time has been covered with sheet ice. It is in general use for coasting purposes and every afternoon sees a number of parties enjoying the sport at that point. . . .

—*The Berkshire Evening Eagle,*
March 12, 1904

FOR YOUR READER'S LOG

How could involvement in a terrible accident change a person's life?

INVESTIGATE
• *What other stories or films have been based on news accounts of actual events?*

Choices: Prologue–Chapter II

Ethan Frome

Building Your Portfolio

SPEAKING AND LISTENING

Who Is That Man?

Starkfield is a small town, and the narrator is an outsider. No doubt the townspeople are as curious about him as he is about Ethan Frome. With a partner, brainstorm what you think two Starkfield residents, such as Harmon Gow and Mrs. Hale, would say to each other about the narrator. What do they know about him? What more would they like to know? What conclusions do they draw about him and his interest in Ethan? Using the information given in the text about the narrator and the local residents, improvise a conversation between the two townspeople about the narrator. Use your imagination and powers of inference to supply information that the text does not provide directly.

READING STRATEGIES

Tracking Sequence of Events

In Chapters I and II, the happiness Ethan feels when he is with Mattie or thinking about her is frequently interrupted or dispelled by inner or outer events. In a small group, fill in a two-column chart to track these changes in Ethan's mood. In the first column, describe what is making Ethan happy or what he is hoping for. In the second column, describe what thought, action, or event changes Ethan's mood.

CREATIVE WRITING

Secret Thoughts

What do you think Mattie feels after her evening dancing with Denis Eady, walking home with Ethan, and meeting the forbidding figure of Zeena at the door? Compose a diary entry that Mattie might write in her room that night, expressing her private hopes, dreams, and fears. Try to write as you imagine Mattie would.

Consider This . . .

The snow had ceased, and a flash of watery sunlight exposed the house on the slope above us in all its plaintive ugliness. The black wraith of a deciduous creeper flapped from the porch, and the thin wooden walls, under their worn coat of paint, seemed to shiver in the wind that had risen with the ceasing of the snow.

What effect does this description of Ethan Frome's house have on you? How does it make you feel about Ethan and his environment? Which words and images make a particularly strong impression?

Writing Follow-up: Personal Reflection

Compose a two- to three-paragraph response to the narrator's description of Ethan's house, expressing how it makes you feel about him and his surroundings. Concentrate on the effects specific words and images have on you, and discuss whether they make you feel more or less sympathetic to Ethan and more or less interested in his story.

Novel Notes

Create an activity based on **Novel Notes, Issue 1.** Here are two suggestions:

- Find a newspaper article that suggests an interesting story to you, and write a brief summary of its main characters and key events.
- Research everyday life in the city of Boston in the late 1800s.

Ethan Frome

First Thoughts

1. On the basis of Ethan and Mattie's behavior during their supper alone together, do you predict that they will manage to change Zeena's plan?

Shaping Interpretations

2. Edith Wharton makes extensive use of visual and tactile **imagery** to contrast how Ethan feels about Mattie with how he feels about Zeena. Find examples of these contrasting images, and discuss what they say about the role each woman plays in Ethan's life.

3. What do we learn in Chapter III about why Mattie comes to the Frome farm? How does this information explain Mattie's attitudes toward Ethan and Zeena?

4. What are the circumstances that first brought Zeena to the Frome farm? How has she changed since her early days there?

5. Silence pervades the novel. When and how does silence first descend on the Frome farm, and when and how is it broken?

6. What kind of man is Andrew Hale? Do you think Ethan had a chance of getting a loan from him? Why or why not?

7. What does the inscription on the gravestone foreshadow for Ethan's future? Which words in particular make an **ironic** comment on Ethan and Zeena's relationship?

Connecting to the Text

8. Ethan looks forward to his supper with Mattie all day, but he also worries that Denis Eady may go to see her while he is away. Have you had an experience like this one, in which you are alternately excited and fearful? What do you think is the cause of such mixed emotions?

Challenging the Text

9. What reason is given for Ethan's marrying Zeena? Do you find this explanation convincing or not? Give reasons based on what you have learned about Ethan's circumstances and character.

Extending the Text

10. What opportunities today would be open to a young woman in Mattie's circumstances that were not open to Mattie?

Writing Opportunity

Present this information in a paragraph that compares and contrasts the two characters. Support your observations with quotations from the novel.

READING CHECK

a. Why does Ethan return home in the middle of the day?

b. What news greets Ethan on his return?

c. How does Ethan feel about Zeena's plan?

d. What is the outcome of Ethan's asking Andrew Hale for a loan?

e. What mars the pleasure of Ethan and Mattie's supper together?

f. How does Ethan manage to restore Mattie's good spirits?

Reading Strategies: Chapters III–IV

Ethan Frome

Evaluating Cause and Effect

A **cause** is what makes something happen. An **effect** is what happens as a result of a cause. Causes and effects may be internal or external.

Complete the following cause-and-effect graphic about the ebb and flow of silence at the Frome farm.

CAUSE	EFFECT
1.	Ethan returns to the farm in the middle of the day.
2. Ethan is left alone on the farm after his father's accident and his mother's "trouble."	
3.	The sound of a human voice returns to the Frome farm.
4.	Zeena grows quiet except to complain.
5. Ethan fails to tell Andrew Hale that he is in serious need of money.	
6.	Mattie and Ethan fall into an awkward silence while alone together.
7. The cat creeps silently up on to the table.	

FOLLOW-UP: Study the relationship between the events outlined in the chart above. On your own paper, write an evaluation of the role of silence in Ethan's life. Consider whether, in Ethan's case, silence is usually associated with negative or positive outcomes.

Chapters III–IV, *Ethan Frome*

REAL OR IMAGINED?

What exactly was the matter with Zeena? Were her illnesses real or imagined? As early as 1913, the medical establishment recognized the symptoms of "nervous prostration" that could result from life on an isolated farm: The early married life of the wives of some of our smaller farmers seems especially calculated to predispose to this condition. Transferred to an isolated farmhouse, very frequently from a home in which she had enjoyed a requisite measure of social and intellectual recreation, she is subjected to a daily routine of very monotonous household labor. Her new home, if it deserves the name, is, by a strict utilitarianism, deprived of everything which can suggest a pleasant thought: not a flower blooms in the garden; books she has, perhaps, but no time to read them. . . .

The urgency of farm work necessitates hurried, unsocial meals, and as night closes in, wearied with his exertions, the farmer is often accustomed to seek his bed at an early hour, leaving his wife to pass the long and lonely evening with her needle. Whilst the disposal of his crops, and the constant changes in the character of farm labor afford her husband sufficient variety and recreation, her daily life, and especially if she have also the unaided care of one or two ailing little children, is exhausting and depressing to a degree of which few are likely to form any correct conception.

—*from* "Observations on a Form of Nervous Prostration,"
Dr. E. H. Van Deusen

INVESTIGATE
- *What does the modern medical establishment say about hysterical illnesses?*

FOR YOUR READER'S LOG

Why might some people feel ill when there is no apparent reason for their symptoms?

In your opinion, how did the isolation of farm life affect Ethan and Zeena?

Life on the Farm

Ethan's farm is a poor place that requires a lot of work. His lot was shared by many. The typical American during the early 1900s lived or worked on a farm or was dependent on farmers. In contrast to rural families in many other parts of the world, the American farm family lived on an isolated farmstead some distance from town and other farm neighbors. In general, the farmstead contained a dwelling, a barn, storage and sheds for small livestock and equipment, a small orchard, and a kitchen garden for vegetables. A woodlot might be found near the house.

Social activity also tended to be widely dispersed among numerous rural churches, schools, or grange halls; the climactic event of the year might well be the county fair, a political rally, or a religious encampment—again at a rural site.

Choices: Chapters III–IV

Ethan Frome

Building Your Portfolio

CREATIVE WRITING

If I Had the Words

At one point during his supper with Mattie, Ethan feels "on the brink of eloquence." What do you imagine Ethan would have said to Mattie if he had not become "paralyzed" at "the mention of Zeena"? Write a monologue for an eloquent Ethan, one who has found words to express his feelings for Mattie as he sits across from her in the warm, bright kitchen.

ART

Hot and Cold

Review the text to see how consistently Wharton uses color and seasonal imagery to contrast the characters of Mattie and Zeena. Mattie is often associated with heat, light, and summer and Zeena with cold, darkness, and winter. Express this contrast in a collage or an abstract painting. Display your artwork along with that of your peers, and discuss the various ways in which you have expressed the same theme.

READING STRATEGIES

Organizing Information

A symbol is a person, place, animal, or object that has meaning that goes beyond its literal or obvious function in a literary work. Winter, for example, stands for or suggests more than just the season in *Ethan Frome*. On your own paper, copy and complete this chart of symbols that appear in Chapters III–IV:

Consider This . . .

For the first time they would be alone together indoors, and they would sit there, one on each side of the stove, like a married couple, he in his stocking feet and smoking his pipe, she laughing and talking in that funny way she had, which was always as new to him as if he had never heard her before.

Whose thoughts and wishes is the narrator expressing?

Writing Follow-up: Comparison and Contrast ▪

In a two- to four-paragraph analysis, compare and contrast the passage above with the actual events of Ethan and Mattie's evening together as they are presented later in Chapters IV and V. Are the fantasies and wishes expressed in the earlier passage realized in the actual unfolding of events? Which parts of the fantasy become actuality, and which do not?

Novel Notes

Create an activity based on **Novel Notes, Issue 2.** Here are two suggestions:

*   Research farm life in different areas of the country during the nineteenth century.
*   List the aspects of Zeena's life that are reflected in the article about nervous illnesses.

Symbol	Literal Function	Symbolic Meaning
1. winter	seasonal setting	lack of love and vitality
2. crimson ribbon		
3. crimping pins		
4. cat		
5.	Zeena's wedding gift	

Ethan Frome

First Thoughts

1. Do you wish that Ethan had kissed Mattie? Why or why not?

Shaping Interpretations

2. What details convey Ethan's sense of well-being as he sits in the kitchen with Mattie?

3. What is done or said to disturb this harmony?

4. The narrator refers to Ethan as having "an illusion" and "being adrift on a fiction." How is Ethan fooling himself?

5. What is Mattie's greatest fear? What does she claim not to fear?

6. What emotions does the mention of sledding arouse in Ethan and Mattie?

7. How does the **mood** change at the end of Chapter V? What is the cause of this change?

8. How is Ethan defeated by circumstances in Chapter VI? Do you think he will be able to overcome the circumstances that stand in the way of his happiness?

9. How does the **motif** of silence recur when Zeena returns?

Challenging the Text

10. Do you think Ethan's happiness the morning after his dinner with Mattie is irrational, as the narrator suggests? Why or why not?

READING CHECK

a. What gives Ethan a momentary shock as he and Mattie sit together in the kitchen?

b. What subject does Ethan raise that upsets Mattie?

c. How do they attempt to restore the harmony between them?

d. What does Ethan remember after Mattie gets up to go?

e. What has happened when Ethan returns from town the next day?

Writing Opportunity

Write your prediction in a paragraph. Support your predictions with facts from the novel.

Name _____ Date _____

Reading Strategies: Chapters V–VI

Ethan Frome

Tracking Plot Complications and Outcomes

In Chapter VI, Ethan, buoyed by the pleasure of being with Mattie the night before, sets himself a definite goal for the day. As the plot unfolds, he is faced with a series of obstacles to achieving his goal.

Use the graphic below to track Ethan's attempts to achieve his goal and the outcomes of his efforts.

Ethan's Goal: _____

_____

Attempts		**Immediate Outcomes**
1. _____	→	_____
2. _____	→	_____
3. _____	→	_____
4. _____	→	_____
5. _____	→	_____

Final Outcome: _____

_____

FOLLOW-UP: Are the obstacles that confront Ethan insurmountable, or are there options that he fails to see or act on? Write your opinion on a separate sheet of paper.

Novel Notes

Novel Notes

Chapters V–VI, *Ethan Frome*

The Puritans

The earliest English settlers in New England were the Puritans, who landed off the coast of Massachusetts in 1620. So great was the influence of the Puritans in the developing country that social historians believe that the American character, especially the New England character, has been shaped by their moral, ethical, and religious convictions.

Who were the Puritans? At home in England, they were Protestants who sought to "purify" the Church of England. When they suffered persecution for their convictions, they fled to Holland and from there to the New World. As many as twenty thousand Puritans would eventually sail to New England.

For the most part they were single-minded visionaries convinced of the rightness of their beliefs. Central to their theology was the belief that original sin had damned most people for eternity. Only the "elect" would be saved, and though there was nothing one could do to win salvation, one could live a life of righteousness and hope for a sign of God's mercy. In their daily lives, then, the Puritans valued self-reliance, industriousness, temperance, and simplicity—values, coincidentally, well suited for farming the rocky soil of New England.

INVESTIGATE
- *What other groups came to this country in search of religious tolerance?*

Edith Wharton

True to Life?

When Edith Wharton wrote her dark and uncompromising picture of farm life in New England, she wished to "draw life as it really was in the derelict mountain villages." She wanted her picture of that life to be "utterly unlike" the work of her predecessor Sarah Orne Jewett. Jewett's stories, with similar settings and poor, rural characters, fairly shine with happiness, light, and hope. Here, in an excerpt from Jewett's *The Country of the Pointed Firs,* the narrator visits a widow living alone. The poor farmland around her has been deserted by the other farmers.

Sarah Orne Jewett

Presently I saw a low gray house standing on a grassy bank close to the road. The door was at the side, facing us, and a tangle of snowberry bushes and cinnamon roses grew to the level of the window-sills. On the doorstep stood a bent-shouldered, little old woman; there was an air of welcome and of unmistakable dignity about her . . . she stood waiting with a calm look until we came near enough to take her kind hand. She was a beautiful old woman, with clear eyes and a lovely quietness and genuineness of manner. . . . Beauty in age is rare enough in women who have spent their lives in the hard work of a farmhouse; but autumnlike and withered as this woman may have looked, her features had kept, or rather gained, a great refinement.

Choices: Chapters V–VI

Ethan Frome

Building Your Portfolio

MUSIC

Capture the Feeling

If you were composing the background music for a film version of *Ethan Frome,* what emotion would you want the music to convey in the following scenes: Ethan seeing Zeena's face in the rocking chair; Ethan kissing the edge of the cloth Mattie is sewing; Ethan hurrying home from town in a downpour; Mattie telling Ethan that Zeena has returned? Discuss your ideas in a group. Then, compose or find appropriate music for one of these scenes, and play it for the class.

CRITICAL WRITING

Fascinating Rhythm

The rhythm of Chapter V is one of recurring opposites, including approach/withdrawal, speech/silence, excitement/fear, hope/despair. Choose two of these pairs, and trace their pattern in the chapter by listing examples of the alternating motifs in a two-column chart. Then, in a brief essay, use the material in your chart to analyze the effect these alternating rhythms and thematic oppositions have on the reader.

PERFORMANCE

On the Ride Back

With a partner, improvise a conversation that could have taken place between Jotham Powell and Zeena as Jotham drives Zeena from the train to the farm. Recall that when Zeena returns, she goes up to her room without saying a word, Jotham refuses to stay for supper, and Ethan worries that Zeena has taken out her grievance on Jotham. Try to keep your dialogue, tone of voice, and gestures as consistent with Wharton's characterization as possible.

Consider This . . .

As they sat thus he heard a sound behind him and turned his head. The cat had jumped from Zeena's chair to dart at a mouse in the wainscot, and as a result of the sudden movement the empty chair had set up a spectral rocking.

What is the symbolic effect of the cat's movement on Ethan and Mattie? What word specifically suggests its symbolic significance?

Writing Follow-up: Cause and Effect ▬

In two to four paragraphs, analyze the effect of the cat's movements on Ethan and Mattie's attempts to become more intimate. Give examples of how the cat literally and figuratively comes between them. Then, discuss who or what the cat seems to symbolize in Chapters V and VI.

Novel Notes

Create an activity based on **Novel Notes, Issue 3.** Here are two suggestions.

- Find more information about the theology of the Puritans in New England.
- Locate other books by Sarah Orne Jewett or her contemporary Mary Wilkins Freeman, and report on their themes.

Ethan Frome

First Thoughts

1. Do you think Zeena is an evil woman, or does she strike you as more sad than bad? Why do you think the pickle dish means so much to her?

Shaping Interpretations

2. What is at the heart of the **conflict** between Zeena and Ethan in the bedroom when Zeena returns from the doctor? Why is Ethan at a disadvantage in this conflict?

3. What emotion that was absent earlier in the marriage **characterizes** the confrontation between husband and wife? Give examples of figurative language that conveys this emotional tone.

READING CHECK

a. What does Zeena announce upon returning from the doctor? What is Ethan's objection to her plan?

b. At first, what does Ethan fail to understand about Zeena's plan?

c. What discovery does Zeena make when she goes to look for her stomach powders?

d. Why does Ethan decide to go see Andrew Hale?

e. What keeps Ethan from carrying out his plan?

Writing Opportunity

Develop your opinion into a paragraph. Provide examples from the novel to support your stance.

---

4. In your opinion, who is the victor in the conflict between Zeena and Ethan? What weapons does the winner use?

5. What emotions alternate in Ethan as he contends with Zeena? What emotions overwhelm him when he is alone with Mattie?

6. How does Mattie react to Zeena's news? What **images** from nature help to characterize her?

7. The theme of deprivation is sounded in Ethan's cry that Zeena has taken everything from him. How do Mattie and Zeena express their own pain at losing what little they have?

8. Ethan is seldom by himself indoors in the story. What does the setting of Ethan's little "study" reveal about his inner life and his private yearnings?

9. What does Mrs. Hale say to Ethan, and what impact do her words have on him? What **internal conflicts** are set off in Ethan by her words?

Challenging the Text

10. Critic Lionel Trilling saw *Ethan Frome* as a story of moral inertia, with a hero so hemmed in by hostile circumstances and so innately passive that he is incapable of making a moral choice. Do you see Ethan's returning home without approaching Mr. Hale as proof of his passivity or as a conscious moral choice? Explain.

Reading Strategies: Chapters VII–VIII

Ethan Frome

Drawing Conclusions

The emotional intensity of *Ethan Frome* is due in large part to the confinement of the three main characters under one roof. Use the triangle below to illustrate the relationships between Ethan, Zeena, and Mattie.

On the outer sides of the triangle, describe the feelings that the character at the beginning of the arrow has for the character at the end of the arrow. Then, do the same for the arrows on the inside of the triangle.

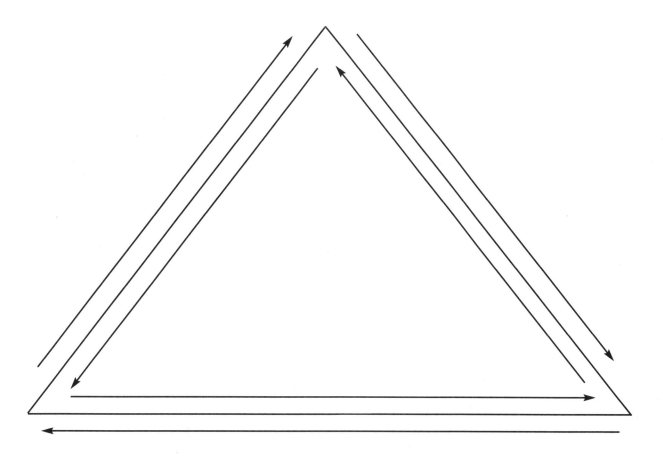

FOLLOW-UP: The triangle displays the feelings of each character for the other two. Whose feelings do you find easiest to understand? Why? Choose one side of the triangle. On your own paper, cite instances in which the feelings described on that side of the triangle are revealed in the novel.

Novel Notes

Chapters VII–VIII, *Ethan Frome*

It's a Hard Life

Why was Mattie willing to take the role of unpaid servant to her cousin Zeena? What kind of life would she face away from the Frome farm? A harsh one, it seems. Poor women like Mattie did not fare well in the cities. In an 1847 article, Carroll D. Wright, director of the Massachusetts Bureau of Statistics of Labor, wrote that young women who worked in shops and factories had to stand all day in poorly ventilated rooms with little light. They were usually not allowed to talk, were given little time for lunch, and suffered a wide variety of health problems, both physical and mental. Wages were low, paying for little more than the bare necessities.

INVESTIGATE

- *What kind of factory work did women of this time perform? Where were the factories located?*

The Shape of the Place

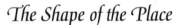

Ethan Frome's house is described by the narrator as "one of those lonely New England farmhouses that make the landscape lonelier." What made Ethan's home look so bleak—even to a stranger unaware of the drama within? According to some, it was the very shape of the place. It lacked the L-shaped addition built onto many farmhouses that connected them to a barn. Farmers could use this addition to enter or leave the house for work without facing the outdoors, a luxury denied to Ethan. Of course, things were even more unwelcoming inside the Frome house. Visitors at the front door found themselves in a low passageway with a ladderlike stairway in front of them. There they waited to be invited to enter a little-used parlor or a humble-looking kitchen. This kitchen, instead of being the warm, comforting center of the house, was shabby and often cold.

Choices: Chapters VII–VIII

Ethan Frome

Building Your Portfolio

ART

Private Spaces

Readers are given a capsule description of the little study to which Ethan retreats in Chapter VIII but are told nothing about Mattie's bedroom. What do you imagine Mattie's room to look like? What treasured possessions does she display, and what do they reveal about her hopes and dreams? Draw or paint your mental picture of Mattie's room, and display it with the work of your classmates. Discuss the similarities and differences in your classmates' visualizations of Mattie's room.

CREATIVE WRITING/ORAL PERFORMANCE

What If?

After Ethan encounters Mrs. Hale, suppose he does ask for money as he planned. What would Ethan say to Mr. Hale? What emotion would be strongest within him: determination, shame, guilt, desperation? How would Mr. Hale respond to Ethan's appeal? Base your response on what you know of Mr. Hale's character. Work with a partner to write the dialogue for such a meeting. Then, after practicing in private, give a dramatic reading of your dialogue for the class.

Consider This . . .

"Confused motions of rebellion stormed in him. He was too young, too strong, too full of the sap of living, to submit so easily to the destruction of his hopes. Must he wear out all his years at the side of a bitter querulous woman? Other possibilities had been in him, possibilities sacrificed, one by one, to Zeena's narrow-mindedness and ignorance."

Do you think this is a fair statement of Ethan's problem? Why or why not? If Zeena is the main obstacle to Ethan's happiness, how might he free himself of her?

Writing Follow-up: Problem and Solution ▬

In a two- to four-paragraph analysis, present the various strategies that Ethan, alone in the cold study, comes up with to escape from Zeena and start a new life with Mattie. Explain why he rejects each idea that comes to him and what solution he adopts the next day. Include your own evaluation of Ethan's situation, indicating whether or not you see any solution to his problem.

Novel Notes

Create an activity based on **Novel Notes, Issue 4.** Here are two suggestions.

- Compare working conditions in stores and factories today with those during Mattie's life.
- Locate other architectural styles for homes during that period, and sketch some of them.

Ethan Frome

First Thoughts

1. Do you agree with Mrs. Hale that Ethan has suffered the most of the three main characters? Give your reasons for agreeing or disagreeing.

Shaping Interpretations

2. Ethan often has trouble separating his wishes and dreams from the realities of his situation. How does this tendency show itself on the day Mattie is due to depart?

3. What is different about the way Mattie and Ethan behave on their ride to the station? What emotion finally overcomes them and determines their actions?

READING CHECK

a. How does Ethan defy Zeena on the day that Mattie leaves the farm?

b. Where do Ethan and Mattie stop on their way to the station? What part do these places play in their history?

c. How do Mattie and Ethan try to prevent their separation?

d. What is the outcome of their resolution?

e. Whose "querulous drone" does the narrator hear in the Frome farmhouse?

4. Are Ethan and Mattie of one mind on School House Hill, or is one character dominating the other? Give reasons for your interpretation.

5. Images of nature have been used in connection with Mattie throughout the novel. Which image in Chapter IX sums up her delicate vulnerability? What is your emotional response to this image?

6. What is ironic about the outcome of Ethan and Mattie's escape plan? What do they achieve and fail to achieve?

7. Describe the scene the narrator witnesses in the Frome farmhouse in the epilogue. What ironic reversal of roles has occurred?

8. What do you think Mattie said to Mrs. Hale that the latter finds so difficult to share with the narrator?

Connecting with the Text

9. What would you have liked to say to Ethan and Mattie before they took that second sleigh ride?

Extending the Text

10. Some reviewers have objected to the cruel resolution of Ethan and Mattie's dilemma, seeing no justification for such a relentlessly tragic tale. Discuss whether you think all literary works should offer a positive message or whether tales of defeat like *Ethan Frome* are also necessary and important.

Writing Opportunity

Write out the conversation that might have taken place between the two women.

Reading Strategies: Chapters IX–Epilogue

Ethan Frome

Making a Story Map

The **structure** of *Ethan Frome* is that of a story within a story. The outer, or frame, story begins in the prologue and concludes in the epilogue. The main, or inner, story is told in the intervening nine chapters.

Use the graphic below to illustrate this structure. List the major events of the frame story in the outer two circles and those of the main story in the inner circle.

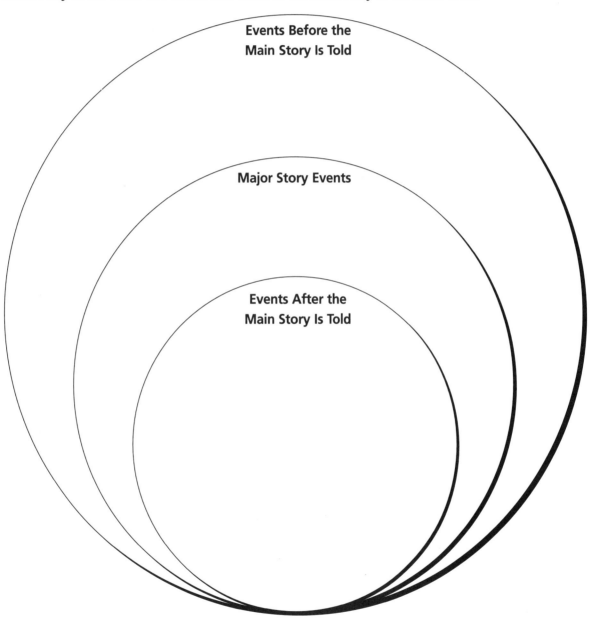

Events Before the
Main Story Is Told

Major Story Events

Events After the
Main Story Is Told

FOLLOW-UP: When do the events of the frame story take place in relation to those of the main story? Some critics believe that Edith Wharton's use of the frame story is awkward and diminishes the impact of the main story. On your own paper, give reasons to explain why you agree or disagree with this opinion.

Tortured Critics

Not all critics reacted favorably to the novel. For some the dark and uncompromising ending was too much. In 1911, a reviewer for *The New York Times* concluded that "torture" was Wharton's goal:

> Mrs. Wharton has, in fact, chosen to build of small crude things and a rude and violent event a structure whose purpose is the infinite refinement of torture. All that is human and pitiful and tender in the tale—and there is much—is designed and contrived to sharpen the keen edge of that torture. And the victims lie stretched upon the rack for twenty years.
>
> —"Three Lives in Supreme Torture,"
> *The New York Times Book Review,*
> October 8, 1911

INVESTIGATE

- *Find some positive critical reactions to Wharton's story.*

FOR YOUR READER'S LOG

Why might people prefer happy endings in the stories they read?

How can a person's name affect the way he or she acts or thinks?

ZENOBIA – QUEEN OF PALMYRA

The Word PLACE

What's in a Name?

Wharton's choice of the name *Zeena* is interesting. Critics have reminded us that Nathaniel Hawthorne chose the name *Zenobia* for a character in his novel *The Blithedale Romance.* His Zenobia is a passionate woman who chooses death when her love is spurned. But the name goes back further than that. Zenobia was also the queen of the Roman colony of Palmyra (present-day Syria) from 267 to 272. She was a strong, powerful ruler who conquered several provinces. Not content with those victories, she led her armies into Egypt and much of Asia Minor—marching farther and farther east until finally meeting defeat at the hands of the Romans.

Choices: Chapters IX–Epilogue

Building Your Portfolio

CRITICAL WRITING

Evaluating the Ending

The critic Doris Grumbach questions Wharton's decision to end the novel with the words of Mrs. Hale. Grumbach suggests that a contemporary novelist might have "let the vision of the three [characters in the kitchen] serve as an ending of great force . . . without the diminishing effect of Mrs. Hale's commonplace summary words." Write your own evaluation of the novel's ending, explaining why you think Wharton's ending is or is not effective. You may also want to discuss alternative endings.

SPEAKING/LISTENING

What's It All About?

Organize a round-table discussion on the theme of *Ethan Frome.* Acting as chair, pose this question to a group of five or six students: Why does Ethan Frome fail to realize his dreams for life and love? To get the discussion started, propose possible answers, such as these: Poverty crushed him. He was overpowered by Zeena's malevolent will. He lacked the assertiveness necessary to find a way out of his difficult circumstances. Then, ask the panel to defend or refute these or other explanations, using evidence from the novel.

CREATIVE WRITING

The Teller of the Tale

We are told little about the narrator, other than that he is working on the construction of a power plant and that he is a man of science, probably an engineer. What else can you infer about him on the basis of his responses to Ethan Frome? Make up a short biography, filling in details about his life before he came to Starkfield and after he left. Include the lesson about life that you think he took from the story of Ethan Frome.

Consider This . . .

"And I say, if she'd [Mattie] ha' died, Ethan might ha' lived; and the way they are now, I don't see's there's much difference between the Fromes up at the farm and the Fromes down in the graveyard; 'cept that down there they're all quiet, and the women have got to hold their tongues."

This is Mrs. Hale's opinion of Ethan's life after the failed suicide. Do you agree with her evaluation?

Writing Follow-up: Persuasion _____ ■

Based on what you have learned about Ethan's character and circumstances, do you think his life would have been very different if Mattie had died in the suicide attempt and he had lived? Do you agree or disagree with Mrs. Hale's characterization of his life as a living death? Like Mrs. Hale, do you sympathize more with Ethan than with the two women? Why or why not? Present your point of view in a persuasive essay, using evidence from the text, history, and your own experience to back up your opinions.

Novel Notes

Create an activity based on **Novel Notes, Issue 5.** Here are two suggestions.

- Find out how many of Wharton's other novels have unhappy endings.
- Locate information about the names given to certain characters in novels you have read or in movies you have seen.

Novel Review

Ethan Frome

MAJOR CHARACTERS

Use the chart below to keep track of the characters in this book. Each time you come across a new character, write the character's name and the number of the page on which the character first appears. Then, jot down a brief description. Add information about the characters as you read. Put a star next to the name of each main character.

NAME OF CHARACTER	DESCRIPTION

FOLLOW-UP: A *dynamic character* changes in some important way as a result of the story's action. In a paragraph, trace the transformation of one dynamic character from the time the character is introduced through the conclusion of the novel.

Novel Review *(cont.)*

Ethan Frome

SETTING

Time ....

Most important place(s) ....

....

One effect of setting on plot, theme, or character ....

....

....

PLOT

List key events from the novel.

- _____   - _____

- _____   - _____

- _____   - _____

Use your list to identify the plot elements below. Add other events as necessary.

Major conflict / problem ....

....

Turning point / climax ....

....

Resolution / denouement ....

....

MAJOR THEMES

- _____

- _____

- _____

Literary Elements Worksheet 1

Ethan Frome

Setting and Characterization

The three **main characters** in the novel are closely associated with specific times of the year or day, with particular places, or with both.

The first column on the left lists the main characters. In the second column, indicate a time (of day or year) or a place that is repeatedly connected with the character in the first column. In the third column, give a quotation from the novel that shows the connection between character and setting.

Characters	Time / Place	Quotation

FOLLOW-UP: Which of the settings listed above is the principal setting of the novel? What is the effect of that setting on the overall mood?

Choose one of the characters, and using the information in the chart, write a short essay explaining how the character's setting reveals and reflects his or her personality.

Literary Elements Worksheet 2

Ethan Frome

Theme

The **theme** is the insight into human life that is revealed in a literary work.

In the center of the web below is one of the themes of the novel. In the attached ovals, write situations or actions that reveal that theme.

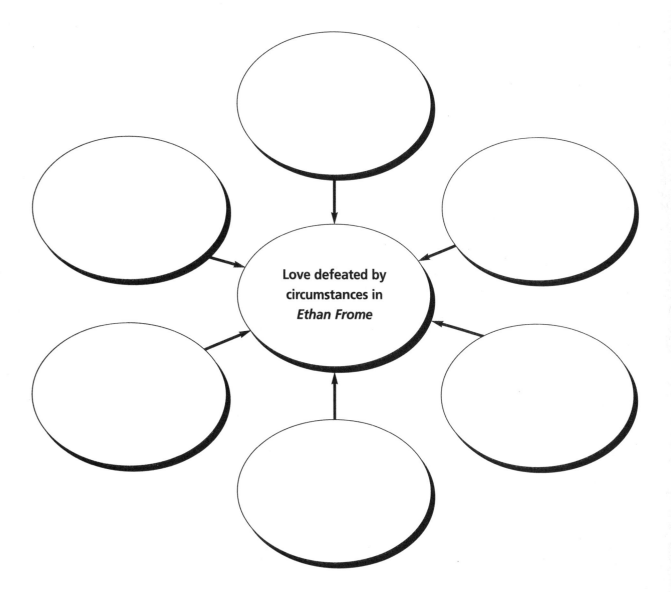

Love defeated by circumstances in *Ethan Frome*

FOLLOW-UP: Create two similar webs on your own paper: one for the theme of love defeated by inertia, or weakness of will, and one for another theme that you see in the novel.

Use the information in one of the webs to write a brief analysis of a major theme in *Ethan Frome* and the insight into human behavior it provides.

Literary Elements Worksheet 3

Ethan Frome

Symbols

Ethan and Mattie's final sleigh ride is a **symbol** of the couple's doomed love. Other aspects of nature and of life in Starkfield and on the Frome farm also have powerful symbolic resonance.

The left side of the chart contains a list of symbols from the novel. In the second column, record an example of the use of each symbol in the text. In the third column, give a brief explanation of the symbolic meaning.

Symbol	Example	Explanation
snow		
porch creeper		
elm tree		
geraniums		
cat		
birds		
pickle dish		

FOLLOW-UP: Which of the symbols do you think is most effective? Why?

How does the symbolism of the pickle dish communicate the themes of deprivation and loss?

Vocabulary Worksheet 1   Prologue–Chapter V

Ethan Frome

A. In the space provided, write the letter of the word or phrase that most nearly defines each word in bold type. (All items are from *Ethan Frome*.)

_____ **1.** After the mortal silence of his long imprisonment Zeena's volubility was music to his ears. *Here the word* **volubility** *means*

    a. complaining   **c.** talkativeness

    b. cheerfulness   **d.** illness

_____ **2.** There was in him a slumbering spark of sociability which the long Starkfield winters had not yet extinguished. *Here the word* **extinguished** *means*

    a. killed   **c.** excited

    b. exaggerated   **d.** frozen

_____ **3.** The cry was balm to his raw wound. *Here the word* **balm** *means*

    a. soothing ointment   **c.** stinging salt

    b. harsh pain   **d.** further insult

_____ **4.** Every one in Starkfield knew him and gave him a greeting tempered to his own grave mien. *Here the word* **mien** *means*

    a. mind   **c.** speech

    b. bearing   **d.** outfit

_____ **5.** During my stay at Starkfield I lodged with a middle-aged widow colloquially known as Mrs. Ned Hale. *Here the word* **colloquially** *means*

    a. occasionally   **c.** informally

    b. respectfully   **d.** temporarily

_____ **6.** The answer sent a pang through him but the tone suffused him with joy. *Here the word* **suffused** *means*

    a. filled   **c.** surprised

    b. shook   **d.** thrilled

_____ **7.** He luxuriated in the sense of protection and authority which his words conveyed. *Here the word* **luxuriated** *means*

    a. doubted   **c.** believed

    b. indulged   **d.** breathed

_____ **8.** On the subject of Ethan Frome I found her unexpectedly reticent. *Here the word* **reticent** *means*

    a. vague   **c.** frank

    b. mean-spirited   **d.** silent

_____ **9.** The builder refused genially, as he did everything else. *Here the word* **genially** *means*

    a. pleasantly   **c.** repeatedly

    b. steadfastly   **d.** sorrowfully

Vocabulary Worksheet 1 (cont.)   Prologue–Chapter V

Ethan Frome

_____10. There was really, even now, no tangible evidence to the contrary. *Here the word* **tangible** *means*

 a. timely   **c.** flimsy

 b. circumstantial   **d.** concrete

B. Write the letter of the *antonym*—the word that is *most nearly opposite* in meaning—for each word in bold type.

_____ 11. **punctually**

 a. unusually   **c.** promptly

 b. irregularly   **d.** suddenly

_____ 12. **innocuous**

 a. immoral   **c.** secure

 b. guilty   **d.** harmful

_____ 13. **eluded**

 a. seized   **c.** outsmarted

 b. oppressed   **d.** escaped

_____ 14. **disdainfully**

 a. respectfully   **c.** cowardly

 b. publicly   **d.** shamefully

_____ 15. **scintillating**

 a. charming   **c.** dull

 b. bright   **d.** scorching

C. Match each word in the left-hand column with its meaning in the right-hand column.

_____ 16. convivial   **a.** degraded

_____ 17. implored   **b.** cheerful

_____ 18. degenerate   **c.** wiped out

_____ 19. languidly   **d.** cheerlessly

_____ 20. effrontery   **e.** listlessly

_____ 21. obliterated   **f.** brashness

_____ 22. countenance   **g.** nonsense

_____ 23. fatuity   **h.** face

_____ 24. disconsolately   **i.** stop

_____ 25. arrest   **j.** begged

Name _____ Date _____

Vocabulary Worksheet 2   Chapters VI–Epilogue

Ethan Frome

A. In the space provided, write the letter of the word or phrase that most nearly defines the word in bold type. (All items are from *Ethan Frome*.)

_____ 1. It was the sense of his helplessness that sharpened his antipathy. *Here the word* **antipathy** *means*
    a. terror   **c.** hatred
    b. anxiety   **d.** sarcasm

_____ 2. Wrath and dismay contended in Ethan. *Here the word* **wrath** *means*
    a. wariness   **c.** despair
    b. hope   **d.** anger

_____ 3. He set his face against the rain and urged on his ponderous pair. *Here the word* **ponderous** *means*
    a. slow-moving   **c.** quick-witted
    b. powerful   **d.** thoughtful

_____ 4. It was neither whining nor reproachful, but dryly resolute. *Here the word* **resolute** *means*
    a. ridiculous   **c.** repetitive
    b. determined   **d.** rousing

_____ 5. Both bowed to the inexorable truth: they knew that Zeena never changed her mind. . . .
    Here the word **inexorable** *means*
    a. unwelcome   **c.** incomparable
    b. unalterable   **d.** eternal

_____ 6. She seldom abbreviated the girl's name, and when she did so it was always a sign of affability.
    Here the word **affability** *means*
    a. friendliness   **c.** anger
    b. forgiveness   **d.** disapproval

_____ 7. Her sombre violence constrained him: she seemed the embodied instrument of fate. *Here the word*
    sombre *means*
    a. sudden   **c.** murderous
    b. grave   **d.** suppressed

_____ 8. With this injunction he left her and went out to the cow-barn. *Here the word* **injunction** *means*
    a. order   **c.** plea
    b. thought   **d.** insult

_____ 9. It was only by incessant labour and personal supervision that Ethan drew a meagre living from his
    land. . . . *Here the word* **incessant** *means*
    a. back-breaking   **c.** time-saving
    b. cheap   **d.** ceaseless

_____ 10. I remained silent, plunged in the vision of what her words evoked. *Here the word* **evoked** *means*
    a. concealed   **c.** recalled
    b. implied   **d.** called forth

Vocabulary Worksheet 2 *(cont.)* Chapters VI–Epilogue

Ethan Frome

B. Write the word from the box that best completes each sentence.

imminent	facetious	devious
ominous	erratic	monotonous
slatternly	transfixed	opaque

11. Zeena's _____ silence the night Ethan walked Mattie home from the dance filled him with dread.

12. Ethan was too concerned about getting back to the farm to pay attention to the _____ remarks of Denis Eady.

13. Ethan grew tired of listening to Zeena's _____ complaints about her health.

14. After the accident, Mattie became as _____ in her appearance as Zeena had been.

15. When their separation was _____, Ethan and Mattie made a fateful decision to die together rather than be parted.

C. Match each word in the left-hand column with its meaning in the right-hand column.

16. aromatic   **a.** comfort

17. audacity   **b.** inflexibility

18. tentatively   **c.** commanded

19. exultantly   **d.** stubborn

20. stolid   **e.** excitedly

21. rigidity   **f.** intensity

22. solace   **g.** poverty-stricken

23. vehemence   **h.** fragrant

24. destitute   **i.** uncertainly

25. adjured   **j.** boldness

Novel Projects

Ethan Frome

Writing About the Novel

ORIGINAL FICTION

While She Was Away

The novel gives no direct account of what Zeena Frome did or felt during the time she was away from home in Bettsbridge, although she makes the results of her visit very clear to Ethan when she returns. Reread Chapters III and VII, which cover Zeena's departure and return, and then compose a chapter recounting her experiences while away. Make your dialogue, events, and characterization as compatible with the novel as you can. Read your chapter to the class.
(Creative Writing)

COMPARE AND CONTRAST

What's in a Name?

The names of the main characters of *Ethan Frome* bring to mind characters from works by Nathaniel Hawthorne. The name Ethan echoes Hawthorne's Ethan Brand, from the short story of the same name. Zeena recalls Zenobia from Hawthorne's novel *The Blithedale Romance*. With a partner, read and research these two works by Hawthorne, taking notes on the similarities and differences between the characters with similar names. Use your notes to write an essay explaining why you think Edith Wharton chose names recalling Hawthorne's characters.
(Critical Writing)

JOURNAL ENTRY

Summer Dreams

Imagine that Ethan wrote a diary in his little study during Mattie's first summer at the Frome farm. Write a series of entries that he might have written during those days when Mattie's presence was brightening his life. Be sure to write an entry for the day of the church picnic, and include Ethan's hopes and dreams as well as his experiences.
(Creative Writing)

COMPARE AND CONTRAST

Rich Versus Poor

Most of Edith Wharton's other fiction is set in turn-of-the-century New York, and her characters are from the wealthy upper crust, the class to which she belonged. *Ethan Frome*, however, breaks that mold. Read one of Wharton's New York novels, such as *The House of Mirth* or *The Age of Innocence*. Then, write an essay comparing and contrasting the setting, the characterization, the themes, and the style of that work with those aspects of *Ethan Frome*.
(Critical Writing)

CRITICAL RESPONSE

A Cinderella Story?

Some critics have called *Ethan Frome* a work of consummate realism, while others, such as Elizabeth Ammons, have pointed out its fairy-tale elements. Zeena, for example, is like a witch or wicked stepmother, and Mattie, a Cinderella who finds her Prince Charming but cannot keep him. Is this novel a realistic depiction of its time and place or a cautionary fairy tale? In an essay, support your opinion with details from the novel.
(Creative/Critical Writing)

LITERARY ANALYSIS

Hopes Dashed

Ethan Frome is a highly ironic novel with very little that turns out as the characters hope or expect, starting with Ethan's marriage. Compose an essay in which you explore the novel's pervasive situational irony. Give specific examples from the text, and discuss how the ironic turns in the plot affect the tone and theme of the novel.
(Critical Writing)

Study Guide **57**

Copyright © by Holt, Rinehart and Winston. All rights reserved.

Cross-Curricular Connections

ART

Picture This!

The wintry New England setting of Wharton's novel is essential to its theme and to the characterization of *Ethan Frome*. Suppose you were the art director in a publishing company and had to choose a painting for the cover of a new edition of *Ethan Frome*. What painting would you choose in order to capture the setting and mood? Work with a small group to research possible artists and their work. Make your choice in collaboration with your peers.

TECHNOLOGY

Way Back Then

The Industrial Revolution of the nineteenth century has barely come to Starkfield. In the novel the railroad is a recent arrival, and electricity is just on the way. At the Frome farm, however, none of these technological improvements have arrived. On the basis of research on preindustrial New England, draw or show illustrations of the methods of heating, lighting, and farming (or saw-milling) that Ethan would have used.

MUSIC

Signature Melodies

Often in an opera, a musical, or a film score, each character in the work has a line of melody, or a musical motif, that signals that character's entrance, aura, or influence. Compose or put together from other pieces of music a musical accompaniment for a scene from *Ethan Frome* in which Ethan, Zeena, and Mattie all appear. Your music should include a motif for each of the three characters and reflect the emotional tone of the scene. Play or perform your composition for the class, and discuss the scene and motifs you chose with your classmates.

SOCIAL STUDIES

Go West, Young Man!

The only escape plan that occurs to Ethan Frome is to take the railroad west. Do some historical research to find out what opportunities or disappointments a poor farmer like Ethan might have encountered in the American West in the 1880s. What kind of work might Ethan have found? What were his chances of acquiring land of his own? What would frontier life have been like for Mattie? Present your findings in an oral or written report.

Multimedia and Internet Connections

NOTE: Check with your teacher about school policies on accessing Internet sites. If a Web site named here is not available, use key words to locate a similar site.

VIDEO: MINISERIES

The Way You See It

Ethan Frome has often been called a cinematic novel, meaning that Edith Wharton creates vivid visual images with her words. Imagine that you are directing a miniseries of the novel for television. What would one episode look like? Work with a production crew of classmates to plan a way to bring some major scenes to the small screen. Create dialogue where necessary, along with sets and costumes. You may want to use a voice-over narrator, but mainly concern yourself with the words and actions of the main characters. Remember to create closing credits, in which you identify yourself and your crew.

FILM: REVIEW

How Does It Rate?

Watch the film version of *Ethan Frome* and compare it with the novel. How do the characters and settings in the film match what you imagined as you were reading? What details were left out, and what details were added or changed? How successful was the filmmaker in transferring the story from the printed page to film? Write a brief review of the film for your classmates, rating it on a scale of 1 to 4, with 1 indicating a first-rate adaptation.

AUDIO: RECORDING

Just Listen

With several classmates, create a reading for a book-on-tape presentation of a section of the novel. Choose an interesting passage of no less than twenty pages,

select readers, and practice reading aloud the dialogue and narration. Listen to a book on tape to get ideas for making your reading an engaging listening experience. Consider sound effects, music, accents, and intonation.

FILM: SET AND COSTUME DESIGN

Age of Opulence

View Martin Scorcese's film adaptation of Edith Wharton's novel *The Age of Innocence* (1993). Take notes on the settings and costumes of this drama of high society in turn-of-the-century New York City. How would the settings and costumes for a movie version of *Ethan Frome* differ? Imagine you are a set and costume designer preparing for a conference with your director. Sketch your ideas for the sets and costumes for two or three key scenes from *Ethan Frome*.

INTERNET SEARCH

Time Travel

Imagine that you have been asked to lead a literary tour of the sites in New York City or western Massachusetts that are associated with Edith Wharton. Using the Internet and other library sources, create an annotated itinerary of places that you could show visitors to inform them about Wharton's life and work. If the actual sites associated with Wharton are not accessible, you may want to show historic photographs or similar sites from the period.

Introducing the Connections

The **Connections** that follow this novel in the HRW Library edition create the opportunity for students to relate the book's themes to other genres, times, and places and to their own lives. The following chart will facilitate your use of these additional works. Succeeding pages offer **Making Meanings** questions to stimulate student response.

Selection	Summary, Connection to Novel
Design **Desert Places** **Storm Fear** Robert Frost *poems*	These poems express the poet's deeply felt emotions about fate, the power of nature, and loneliness—themes expressed in the novel.
The Snow Man Wallace Stevens *poem*	According to the speaker, only a person with a "mind of winter" can contemplate the season without being affected by its bleak emptiness.
The Stone Boy Gina Berriault *short story*	The silence that pervades the Frome household kills all hope of change or happiness. In this short story a young boy accidentally shoots his brother. The silence that comes with grief paralyzes the family, who, unable to express their feelings about the tragedy, are never able to deal with it.
The Angry Winter Loren Eiseley *essay*	During a walk on a November day, the sight of the cemetery of a "long vanished" community brings to mind our mortality.
The Hiltons' Holiday Sarah Orne Jewett *short story*	This story of a poor New England farm family and the pleasure they find in a simple day's holiday is a sharp contrast to the darker effects of poverty and hard times in *Ethan Frome*.

Introducing the Connections *(cont.)*

Selection	Summary, Connection to Novel
*from **Ethan Frome** as **Fairy Tale*** Elizabeth Ammons *critical essay*	This critic proposes reading *Ethan Frome* as a fairy tale, similar to the tale of "Snow White," with Ethan as Mattie's hapless Prince Charming. Sadly, there is no happily ever after for Mattie/Snow White in the novel.
*from **A Backward Glance*** Edith Wharton *essays*	In a memoir, Edith Wharton takes a look back at how she came to write *Ethan Frome.*
Edith Wharton: A Biography R.W.B. Lewis *biographical excerpt*	Most reviewers recognize *Ethan Frome* as one of Wharton's finest achievements, but many find the uncompromising ending too terrible to accept. This critic considers the novel, with its bleak conclusion, a classic example of literary realism in the spirit of Wharton's predecessor Nathaniel Hawthorne.

Exploring the Connections

Making Meanings

Connecting with the Novel

Which of the three poems best reflects the tone of the novel?

1. What words would you use to describe the **mood** or **tone** of each poem?

2. What does "Design" say about the choices we have in life? Do you agree with this view?

3. What questions is the speaker in "Storm Fear" asking?

READING CHECK

What scenes or activities do the speakers in the poems describe?

The Snow Man

Connecting with the Novel

How does the phrase "a mind of winter" relate to the character of Ethan?

1. Who is the "snow man" referred to in the title?

2. What are the possible meanings of the phrase "one must have a mind of winter"?

3. The word *nothing* is referred to three times in the final stanza. What is the significance of each reference?

4. Describe the **mood** and **tone** of the poem. How do the sensory images in the poem contribute to that mood and tone? How do they reinforce the theme that is expressed in the final line?

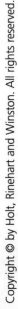

Exploring the Connections (cont.)

Making Meanings

The Stone Boy

Connecting with the Novel

What elements of this story echo the mood and theme of *Ethan Frome*?

1. List details in the story that convey how Arnold feels about his older brother.

2. "It was then that he had felt his father and the others set their cold, turbulent silence against him." How does that silence divide the characters in the story? Could it have been otherwise?

3. Explain the **symbolic significance** of the title of the story.

4. If you were telling the events of the story to someone, how would you explain Arnold's actions after the accident? What do you think was happening to him?

READING CHECK

a. What accident sets the story in motion?

b. What does Arnold do after the accident?

c. What does the sheriff decide about the accident?

The Angry Winter

Connecting with the Novel

What connections can you see between Eiseley's musings on the desolation of life and Ethan's life?

1. What does the writer admire about the rabbit?

2. What ideas does the writer suggest when he says that man is a "belated phantom of the angry winter"? What meaning can you make of the last sentence?

READING CHECK

a. What decision did the creator make about immortality for man?

b. What animal does the writer see in the country?

c. What has happened to the community that placed the cemetery where the narrator finds it?

Making Meanings

The Hiltons' Holiday

Connecting with the Novel

This story is a stark contrast to *Ethan Frome*. List some of the differences.

1. How do the people the Hiltons meet in town—Judge Masterson, the clerk in the dry-goods store, the old man—react to the family? What can you infer about the values of the community from these reactions?

2. How did each character in the Hilton family respond to the day? What do their responses tell you about them?

READING CHECK

a. What happened to the Hiltons' son?

b. Why does Mrs. Hilton stay home?

c. How did Mr. Hilton come to know Judge Masterson?

3. Some stories leave us feeling that there is more to tell. What do you see in the future for the Hilton family? What do you think the girls will do when they grow up?

from Ethan Frome *as Fairy Tale*

Connecting with the Novel

What other fairy tales remind you of this novel? How would you have to change the ending of the novel to make it more like a fairy tale?

1. Contrast Zeena's appearance with Mattie's. According to the essay, how do the two characters correspond in appearance to their fairy-tale roles?

2. What are some images Ethan associates with Mattie Silver? According to the essay, how do those images affect his actions?

READING CHECK

a. What fairy tale does the author say the novel resembles?

b. What three roles do Ethan, Zeena, and Mattie take from that fairy tale?

c. How do the endings differ?

3. What is Zeena's purpose in the fairy-tale plot? How does she achieve it?

Making Meanings

from *A Backward Glance*

Connecting with the Novel

How would you respond to critics of the novel?

1. What does Edith Wharton say about why she chose the **story-within-a-story structure** for *Ethan Frome?*

2. According to Wharton, why did the making of *Ethan Frome* bring her "the greatest joy"?

3. What roles did Edith Wharton intend Mrs. Hale and Harmon Gow to play in the narrative?

READING CHECK

Briefly state the main idea of each essay.

from *Edith Wharton: A Biography*

Connecting with the Novel

Do you share the view that the ending of the novel is "too terrible to be borne"?

1. Lewis writes that Edith Wharton may have based *Ethan Frome* on events in her own life. According to that view, what changes did she make to create her characters?

2. Lewis writes that the grim story is "a classic of the realistic genre." Do you find the story realistic? Why or why not?

READING CHECK

Summarize Lewis's ideas about the internal and external influences that contributed to the writing of *Ethan Frome.*

Name _____ Date _____

TEST   PART I: OBJECTIVE QUESTIONS

In the space provided, mark each true statement *T* and each false statement *F.* (10 points)

_____ **1.** According to the narrator, Ethan Frome is the most striking figure he sees at the local post office.

_____ **2.** Ethan was forced to marry Zeena to please his dying mother.

_____ **3.** Ethan was a man without ambition or dreams for a better life.

_____ **4.** It was Mattie's idea to steer the sled straight for the big elm tree.

_____ **5.** After the accident, Mattie remained as sweet natured as ever.

Circle the letter of the answer that best completes the statement. *(20 points)*

6. The action of *Ethan Frome* takes place in or near
- **a.** Starkfield
- **b.** Bettsbridge
- **c.** Boston
- **d.** Corbury Junction

7. The Frome house and farm can best be described as
- **a.** prosperous
- **b.** picturesque
- **c.** poor
- **d.** promising

8. Ethan is frequently associated with images of
- **a.** sun and warmth
- **b.** ice and snow
- **c.** birds and trees
- **d.** illness and medicine

9. The narrator first learns that Ethan has been in a "smashup" from
- **a.** Mrs. Hale
- **b.** Mattie Silver
- **c.** Zeena Frome
- **d.** Harmon Gow

10. Zeena first comes to the Frome farm when Ethan's mother is
- **a.** gravely ill
- **b.** lonely
- **c.** burdened with work
- **d.** young and fit

11. Zeena Frome is preoccupied with
- **a.** money matters
- **b.** local gossip
- **c.** her appearance
- **d.** her health

TEST · PART I: OBJECTIVE QUESTIONS *(cont.)*

12. While away from home seeing a new doctor, Zeena arranges for

    a. an operation

    b. a hired girl

    c. a mortgage on the farm

    d. new clothes and furniture

13. Ethan decides not to ask Andrew Hale for a loan because he feels

    a. guilty and ashamed

    b. hopeful

    c. carefree and irresponsible

    d. too proud to ask

14. Ethan and Mattie are permanently injured as a result of

    a. an assault by Zeena

    b. a plunge into an icy pond

    c. a sledding accident

    d. being caught in a blizzard

15. Which of the following is an important theme of *Ethan Frome?*

    a. Love conquers all.

    b. All love is an illusion.

    c. Circumstances can defeat a person.

    d. Only the strong survive.

TEST PART II: SHORT-ANSWER QUESTIONS

Answer each question, using the lines provided. *(40 points)*

16. What structural device is used to tell the story? How does it affect the time setting of the novel?

_____

_____

_____

17. Briefly explain the imagery of light and dark in the novel, and tell with whom those images are associated.

_____

_____

_____

18. What circumstances brought Mattie Silver to the Frome farm? How does she feel about being there?

_____

_____

_____

19. What kind of person is Mattie? Describe her effect on Ethan.

_____

_____

_____

20. What are some of the external obstacles that prevent Ethan from realizing his dreams?

_____

_____

_____

21. What are some of the internal conflicts that trouble Ethan?

_____

_____

_____

Name _____ Date _____

 **PART II: SHORT-ANSWER QUESTIONS** *(cont.)*

22. What reasons does Zeena give for sending Mattie away? What do you think is her real reason?

_____

_____

_____

23. Illness and physical injuries are repeated motifs in the novel. Which characters suffer from these maladies? Does anyone recover?

_____

_____

_____

24. Explain the final irony in Ethan and Mattie's effort to stay together.

_____

_____

_____

25. What role reversal is revealed in the epilogue of the novel?

_____

_____

_____

TEST | PART III: ESSAY QUESTIONS

Choose two of the following topics. Use your own paper to write two or three paragraphs about each topic you choose. *(30 points)*

a. Give your interpretation of Ethan Frome's **character.** Do you see him, for example, as a hero, a victim, or a flawed man undone by his own limitations?

b. Discuss Wharton's use of **symbols** in *Ethan Frome.* Cite two or three symbols, and explain their meaning.

c. Explain how the **setting** of *Ethan Frome* reflects and reinforces **characterization** and **theme.**

d. Evaluate the use of the **first-person narrator**

and the **frame structure** of the novel. Support your opinion on the effectiveness of those devices with evidence from the text.

e. Illustrate the development of a particular **theme** (for example, thwarted love) throughout the novel. Trace the theme through the characterization, events, and symbolism.

f. Discuss how one of the **Connections** (in the HRW Library edition of *Ethan Frome*) is related to a theme, issue, or character in the novel.

Use this space to make notes.

Answer Key

Answer Key

Prologue–Chapter II

■ Making Meanings

READING CHECK

a. He sees Ethan Frome in the post office in the town of Starkfield, Massachusetts.

b. He talks to local people, including Harmon Gow and his landlady, Mrs. Ned Hale, about Ethan.

c. He finds out that Ethan Frome was in a "smashup" with a companion.

d. Orphaned and penniless, Mattie has come to help "sickly" Zeena with the housework.

e. Ethan and Mattie share a love of natural beauty.

f. She suggests that Mattie might leave the farm to marry Denis Eady.

---

1. Students should provide details about Ethan's appearance and behavior to support their responses.

2. He is a "striking figure," although "the ruin of a man." He was tall, with a "careless powerful look." He was lame, stiff, and "grizzled." "There was something bleak and unapproachable in his face." He looked older than his years and had a red gash across his forehead. He was grave and silent. The narrator is impressed, disturbed, and intensely curious about Ethan Frome.

3. He concludes that although the Fromes are tough, Ethan has been worn down by too many winters in Starkfield and by always having to care for others.

4. The narrator first mentions winter in connection with Ethan. Winter, here, has overtones of unrelenting hardship that wears away at a man, even a tough one.

5. Mrs. Hale, reacting with pained reticence, is reluctant to speak about an event she describes as "awful." Her reluctance mirrors Ethan's silent suffering.

6. Images include "a square of light trembled," "low unlit passage," "rose into obscurity," and "line of light . . . sent its ray across the night." Light struggles to overcome darkness, but darkness prevails. The narrator has an auditory experience. He hears "a woman's voice droning querulously."

7. Mattie is in love with Ethan but dares not express her love, even to herself. Her behavior, however, reveals her feelings. She turns down a ride with Denis Eady, walks arm in arm with Ethan, and gets visibly upset at talk about her leaving the farm.

8. Zeena is probably jealous of the warmth and intimacy she senses between Ethan and Mattie. She wants to get back at Ethan for neglecting her.

9. Many students will have difficulty feeling sympathy for Zeena because she is self-centered and cold. Others may feel sympathetic when they consider her isolation, her poverty, and Ethan's dutiful but indifferent attitude toward her.

10. Sample response: Although most people in love experience emotional ups and downs, Ethan probably has more obstacles in the way of fulfilling his dream of love than most other young men. His marriage to Zeena and his poverty, for example, are two external circumstances that will be difficult for him to overcome. His own lack of assertiveness may also get in his way.

■ Reading Strategies Worksheet
Understanding Characterization
Responses will vary. Sample responses follow.

Ethan at Twenty-eight: strong, energetic, curious, sensitive, full of hopes and desires he finds hard to express

Ethan at Fifty-two: lame, gash on face, grave, silent, bleak

Traits That Remain Unchanged: dutiful, dependable, stoical, inexpressive

FOLLOW-UP: Students should base their summaries on the information they compile in their diagrams. They should say how much or how little Ethan Frome has changed over the years. Most students will conclude that Ethan's basic character does not change much over the years.

Chapters III–IV

■ Making Meanings

READING CHECK

a. He is worried by his wife's silence and Mattie's uneasiness the night before and wants to be home in case of trouble.

b. Zeena is ready to go on an overnight journey to see a new doctor.

c. He is happy to get the opportunity to be alone with Mattie.

d. Hale refuses Ethan's request.

e. The cat breaks a favorite pickle dish of Zeena's, which Mattie is using without her permission.

f. Ethan promises to glue the pieces of the dish back together and replace it before Zeena discovers it is broken.

1. Students should provide details about the characters to support their predictions.

2. Mattie is associated with light, warmth, softness, and color; Zeena, with darkness, cold, hardness, and absence of color. The rays from Mattie's candle send light into the "perfectly black" room Ethan shares with Zeena. Mattie's face is "part of the sun's red." Zeena's face, in pale light reflected off a snowbank, is "drawn and bloodless." Zeena's dress is brown, her bonnet stiff, and her hair thin and crimped. In contrast, Mattie is radiant in the lustrous lamplight, her dark hair trimmed with a crimson ribbon, and her gait "soft and flowing." Mattie is a source of beauty, joy, and love to Ethan, while Zeena represents the absence of all those life-giving qualities.

3. Mattie comes to the farm a penniless orphan after her dishonest father dies, leaving huge debts, and her mother dies in disgrace. Without relatives willing to help, she tries supporting herself as a stenographer and shopgirl but has neither the skills nor the stamina to succeed. Because she is helpless and lacking options, she feels grateful for a home and fears displeasing Zeena.

4. Zeena came to nurse Ethan's mother when the old woman was dying. She was lively and efficient and freed Ethan to concentrate on his farm and mill work. Later she became silent, except when complaining, obsessed with her health, and a burden to Ethan rather than a help.

5. Silence begins after his father's accident, when Ethan's mother, who was once "a talker," falls strangely quiet; the silence lasts for years, until Zeena comes to nurse the dying Mrs. Frome.

6. Andrew Hale is a genial man, inclined to spend money to make others happy. Students may argue that such a man would have probably lent Ethan money if he had known of his genuine need. Others may say that Mr. Hale had no ready cash to lend Ethan, so it would not have mattered how Ethan approached him.

7. The inscription foreshadows a long marriage for Ethan and Zeena. The name Endurance calls ironic attention to Zeena's unstoical tendency to complain about her health and seek relief in the form of medicines, doctors, and household help. The word *peace* ironically underscores the chilly silence that passes for marital harmony between Ethan and Zeena.

8. Responses will vary, and students need not share their experiences unless they wish to. Mixed emotions may be explained by uncertainty in the face of the unknown or by lack of confidence due to youth or inexperience.

9. Ethan marries Zeena because he is afraid to spend the winter alone in the quiet, isolated

farmhouse. Many students will find this explanation convincing because Ethan has been so lonely for so long, and Zeena does appear to offer company and efficient household management.

10. Young women today could seek public or private assistance and job training. They also would have the benefit of a free public education through high school. The variety of jobs open to women has also expanded greatly since Mattie's day.

■ Reading Strategies Worksheet

Evaluating Cause and Effect

Responses will vary. Sample responses follow.

1. Ethan is disturbed by Zeena's silence the night before.

2. Ethan has no time to socialize, and silence overcomes him and the household.

3. Zeena comes to nurse Ethan's dying mother.

4. Zeena grows unhappy with life on the farm and with Ethan, who never listens to her.

5. Andrew Hale does not give Ethan the money.

6. Zeena's name is mentioned.

7. The pickle dish crashes to the floor.

FOLLOW-UP: Most students will conclude that silence has a generally negative impact on Ethan's life, whether it is a cause or an effect. When expression replaces silence, Ethan is usually happier and more effective.

Chapters V–VI

■ Making Meanings

> **READING CHECK**
> a. When Mattie sits in Zeena's rocker, he fleetingly "sees" Zeena's face instead of Mattie.
> b. He talks about Mattie's getting married soon.
> c. They resolve not to talk about Zeena.
> d. He remembers that he did not even touch Mattie's hand.
> e. Zeena has returned and gone upstairs without saying a word.

1. Many students will think they should have kissed, while others will think it would have been a mistake since the two have no future together.

2. He sits near the fire and smokes his pipe while Mattie sews in the lamplight. He feels "lazy and light of mood," as if "in another world, where all was warmth and harmony and time could bring no change."

3. Disturbances include Ethan's seeing Zeena's face when Mattie sits in the rocker, conversation about Ned and Ruth's possible marriage, the possibility of Mattie getting married, and Zeena's feelings toward Mattie.

4. Ethan is allowing himself to forget that his intimacy with Mattie cannot continue since his wife will be returning the next day.

5. Mattie is afraid of Zeena's displeasure and, by inference, of Zeena's sending her away. She professes not to be afraid of coasting with Ethan down the hill.

6. The topic of sledding arouses feelings of romantic adventure, excitement, and cozy intimacy in the couple and, in Ethan, a sense of male mastery and protectiveness toward Mattie.

7. The mood changes from glowing excitement to listless weariness when the couple realize that their intimacy will end with Zeena's return.

8. An injured horse, bad weather, and slow clerks in the stores prevent Ethan from mending the dish or having time alone with Mattie before Zeena's return. Most students will have a sense of the relentless move toward tragedy that characterizes Ethan's story.

9. Mattie whispers to Ethan that Zeena has returned. Zeena goes upstairs without saying a word. Jotham Powell laconically refuses an invitation to stay for dinner. Ethan and Mattie look at each other silently over the supper table.

10. Some may say that Ethan's happiness is irrational because it cannot last; others may say that love and happiness are to be cherished whether or not they last.

■ Reading Strategies Worksheet

Tracking Plot Complications and Outcomes
Responses will vary. Sample responses follow.

Ethan's Goal: to bring wood to town, buy glue, and get home to mend the dish before Zeena returns

Attempts and Immediate Outcomes: **1.** goes to wood lot to pick up wood ⟶ horse slips on ice and cuts its knee **2.** loads the sledge with wood ⟶ sleety rain slows work down **3.** in town quickly unloads the wood ⟶ works like ten men **4.** tries to buy glue quickly ⟶ Denis Eady can't find glue, and Mrs. Homan dawdles finding it **5.** drives home with glue ⟶ steady rain delays horse

Final Outcome: Zeena is home before Ethan, and the dish has not been mended.

FOLLOW-UP: Opinions will vary, but if students see other options for Ethan, they should provide specific examples from the text, history, or their own experience. If they see the obstacles he faces as insurmountable, they should explain why.

Chapters VII–VIII

■ Making Meanings

READING CHECK
- **a.** Zeena has arranged for a hired girl to take over all the housework so she can rest completely. Ethan objects because he cannot afford to pay her wages.
- **b.** At first, Ethan doesn't realize that Zeena plans to send Mattie away.
- **c.** She finds the broken pickle dish.
- **d.** He plans to ask for money so he and Mattie can get away.
- **e.** He feels guilty and cannot bring himself to lie and take advantage of good people like the Hales.

1. Responses will vary. Students should provide details about Zeena and about her hard life on the farm to support their opinions of her. Most will recognize that for Zeena the dish symbolizes beauty and the hope of love.

2. Zeena wants Mattie to go, and Ethan wants her to stay. Since Mattie is Zeena's relative, Zeena has more say in Mattie's going or staying than Ethan. Also, Ethan has to be careful to hide his feelings for Mattie.

3. The confrontation is an openly angry one, as shown in similes, such as "senseless and savage as a physical fight," "pause in the struggle, as though the combatants were testing their weapons," and "his wife's retort was like a knife-cut across the sinews."

4. Zeena is the clear winner, making successful use of psychological weapons. She cleverly uses her illness as a pretext for getting rid of Mattie, making it difficult for Ethan to object without appearing insensitive to her pain and suffering.

5. Ethan oscillates between wrath and dismay, defiance and helplessness. With Mattie he feels overwhelming physical desire and protective tender-

ness, along with sadness and fear at the thought of their separation.

6. Mattie is terrified of being sent away. Her vulnerability is highlighted by images such as "her lashes beat his cheek like netted butterflies" and "drooping before him like a broken branch."

7. Zeena is indignant, resentful, and heartbroken when she discovers the broken pickle dish, which reveals the lack of love in her marriage and the lack of beauty in her life, as well as her own withholding nature. Mattie becomes desperate and frightened when she finds out she has to leave; she is reminded that she has little money, no other family or friends, and no skills.

8. The study reveals Ethan's yearnings for knowledge, self-expression, and contact with people with similar interests and aspirations.

9. Mrs. Hale sympathizes with Ethan because of the hard life he has had taking care of his wife and his mother. Ethan is deeply moved by this rare acknowledgment of his suffering. His sense of duty and his revulsion at deceiving and using good people like the Hales are in conflict with his desire to escape with Mattie.

10. Responses will vary, but students should be able to support their opinions with details and quotations from the novel.

■ Reading Strategies Worksheet

Drawing Conclusions

Responses will vary. Sample responses follow.

Ethan for Zeena: anger, fear, compassion, responsibility

Ethan for Mattie: love, attraction, tenderness, protectiveness

Zeena for Ethan: disappointment, resentment, frustration, vindictiveness

Zeena for Mattie: jealousy, hatred, resentment, vindictiveness

Mattie for Ethan: love, admiration, gratitude, compassion

Mattie for Zeena: fear, shame, dependency

FOLLOW-UP: Sample responses: Ethan's negative feelings for Zeena are the easiest to understand because she is so self-centered, unattractive, and disagreeable.

Ethan's anger and fear of Zeena are displayed in the scene in their bedroom when he tries but fails to convince her that he cannot afford a hired girl and that a poor girl like Mattie should not be sent out to work among strangers. Zeena's vindictiveness is displayed in the clever way she traps Ethan by playing on his compassion and sense of duty.

Chapters IX–Epilogue

■ Making Meanings

> **READING CHECK**
> a. He will not be deterred from driving Mattie to the station, even though Zeena insists she go with Jotham Powell.
> b. They stop off at Shadow Pond, where they enjoyed themselves on a summer picnic, and at School House Hill, where they meant to go coasting but never did.
> c. They agree to seek death together by sledding straight into the elm at the bottom of School House Hill.
> d. They hit the tree, but instead of dying, they end up crippled and under Zeena's thumb for the rest of their lives.
> e. Mattie is the source of the "querulous drone."

1. Most students will feel the most sympathy for Mattie, not for Ethan; some may think that his life at the end is the more tragic.

2. Before they leave home, Ethan finds it hard to believe that Mattie is really going ("the sense of unreality overcame him once more"), and on the ride to the station, he seems able to laugh and

convince himself that they still have a lot of time left together.

3. During their ride, Mattie and Ethan express their love more openly than ever before, both verbally and physically. They are finally overcome with the hopelessness about their situation.

4. Responses will vary. Many students will interpret the couple's suicide pact as a mutual one, even though Mattie initially proposes the plan.

5. "He heard a little animal twittering somewhere near by under the snow. It made a small frightened *cheep* like a field mouse, and he wondered languidly if it were hurt." Responses to the image may include shock, compassion, sadness, or a sense of futility.

6. The couple hope to avoid the pain of separation by dying together. They fail to die, and the togetherness they achieve turns out to be a joyless bondage, a slow sentence of death rather than a quick end to their suffering.

7. In a gloomy, sparsely furnished kitchen, the narrator sees two poorly dressed women—one short and dark eyed, huddled immobile by the fire, and the other taller and bonier, moving about the cold room. The seated one, Mattie Silver, who once waited on the complaining invalid Zeena, is now issuing complaints to a reenergized Zeena, who is functioning as Mattie's caretaker.

8. Many may conjecture that Mattie expressed a wish to have died in the smashup.

9. Many students may choose to assert the value of life over death.

10. Responses will vary. Students may argue that to be true to life, literature must deal with defeat and despair as well as victory and hope.

■ Reading Strategies Worksheet

Making a Story Map

Responses will vary. Sample responses follow.

Events Before the Main Story Is Told

1. The narrator sees Ethan Frome at the Starkfield post office.

2. The narrator gets information about Ethan from Harmon Gow and Mrs. Hale.

3. The narrator is caught in a snowstorm with Ethan and is invited to stay overnight at the Frome farm.

Main Story Events

1. Ethan Frome falls in love with Mattie, who has come to help his ailing wife, Zeena.

2. A resentful Zeena forces Mattie to leave by employing a hired girl.

3. Hindered by poverty, Ethan cannot find a way to keep Mattie or go away with her.

4. The couple decide to die together by coasting into a tree, but they survive, crippled for life and under the same roof with Zeena.

Events After the Main Story Is Told

1. While entering the Frome kitchen, the narrator hears a complaining female voice.

2. Inside he sees two haggard women: The complaining one is identified by Ethan as Mattie Silver; the active one, as Zeena Frome.

3. Mrs. Hale describes Ethan's life with the two women as worse than death.

FOLLOW-UP: The events of the frame story take place twenty-four years after those of the main story.

Students' opinions on the effectiveness of the frame story will vary. Some students may think the device is distracting and confusing, especially since so little is told about the narrator.

Answer Key (cont.)

Literary Elements Worksheet 1

■ Setting and Characterization

Responses will vary. Sample responses are listed.

Character	Time/Place	Quotation
Ethan	winter, farmhouse, New England	"Guess he's been in Starkfield too many winters." (Prologue)
		"to see in the diminished dwelling the image of his own shrunken body" (Prologue)
Mattie	summer, outdoors	"Her face changed with each turn of their talk, like a wheatfield under a summer breeze."
		"her voice . . . a rustling covert leading to enchanted glades" (Chapter V)
Zeena	darkness, indoors, bedroom	"Against the dark background of the kitchen, she stood up tall and angular." (Chapter II)
		"The room was almost dark, but in the obscurity he saw her sitting by the window, bolt upright." (Chapter VII)

FOLLOW-UP: The principal setting is winter in New England. The effect of this setting is a bleak, chilling mood.

A successful essay will use the specific connections between the individual and the setting to make generalizations about the character's overall personality.

■ Theme

Responses will vary. Sample responses are listed.

Love Defeated by Circumstances in Ethan Frome

Cat breaks Zeena's prize dish.

Weather keeps Ethan from returning on time with glue.

Zeena finds the broken dish.

Ethan and Mattie injure rather than kill themselves.

FOLLOW-UP: Responses will vary. Examples of Ethan's defeat by inertia include his marriage to Zeena to stave off loneliness, his failure to obtain money from Andrew Hale, his tendency to escape into fantasy, his inability to devise a plan of escape from Zeena, and his compliance with Mattie's proposal that they kill themselves.

Successful completion of the essay requires not only tracing the theme throughout the novel but also commenting on its application to human behavior in general.

■ Symbols

Responses will vary. Sample responses are listed.

Symbol	Example	Explanation
snow	"The snow began to fall again,	confusion, mystery,

Symbol	Example	Explanation
	cutting off our last glimpse of the house. . . ." (Prologue)	loss
creeper	"The black wraith of a deciduous creeper flapped from the porch." (Prologue)	death, gloom, decay
elm tree	"The big elm thrust out a deadly elbow." (Chapter IX)	menace, death, fate
geraniums	"She . . . lifted two of the geranium pots in her arms, moving them away from the cold window." (Chapter V)	life-giving nurture, warmth, cheerfulness, vitality (associated with Mattie)
cat	"jumped up into Zeena's chair, rolled itself into a ball, and lay watching them with narrowed eyes" (Chapter V)	retribution, guilt, conscience (associated with Zeena)
birds	"Once, in the stillness, the call of a bird in a mountain ash was so like her laughter that his heart tightened and then grew large." (Chapter VIII)	beauty, delicacy, love, vulnerability (associated with Mattie)
pickle dish	"In her hands she carried the	deprivation, loss,

Symbol	Example	Explanation
	fragments of the red glass pickle dish." (Chapter VII)	possessiveness, shattered dreams (associated with Zeena)

FOLLOW-UP: Responses will vary. Sample answer: The pickle dish, a bright bauble of little intrinsic worth, is Zeena's most prized possession, illustrating how little she has or ever had. Because it was a wedding present, the dish also represents her attachment to Ethan, which, however limited, is another one of her few possessions, and it, too, has been shattered by Mattie.

Vocabulary Worksheets

If you wish to score these worksheets, assign the point values given in parentheses.

■ Vocabulary Worksheet 1

Prologue–Chapter V

A. *(4 points each)*

1.	c. talkativeness	6.	a. filled
2.	a. killed	7.	b. indulged
3.	a. soothing ointment	8.	d. silent
4.	b. bearing	9.	a. pleasantly
5.	c. informally	10.	d. concrete

B. *(4 points each)*

11. b. irregularly
12. d. hurtful
13. a. seized
14. a. respectfully
15. c. dull

C. *(4 points each)*

16.	b. cheerful	21.	c. wiped out
17.	j. begged	22.	h. face
18.	a. degraded	23.	g. nonsense
19.	e. listlessly	24.	d. cheerlessly
20.	f. brashness	25.	i. stop

■ Vocabulary Worksheet 2

Chapter VI–Epilogue

A. *(4 points each)*

1. c. hatred
2. d. anger
3. a. slow-moving
4. b. determined
5. b. unalterable
6. a. friendliness
7. b. grave
8. a. order
9. d. ceaseless
10. d. called forth

B. *(4 points each)*

11. ominous
12. facetious
13. monotonous
14. slatternly
15. imminent

C. *(4 points each)*

16. h. fragrant
17. j. boldness
18. i. uncertainly
19. e. excitedly
20. d. stubborn
21. b. inflexibility
22. a. comfort
23. f. intensity
24. g. poverty-stricken
25. c. commanded

Exploring the Connections

■ Design
Desert Places
Storm Fear

> **READING CHECK**
>
> In "Design" the speaker describes a moth trapped by a spider. The scene in "Desert Places" is a snow-covered field. "Storm Fear" describes the violence of a winter storm.

1. Students should use words like *somber* and *lonely* to describe the mood in all three poems. They should note that there is a fatalistic tone in all three.

2. Most students may feel that the poem is suggesting that we have no choices or that the ones we have are not true choices. Some students may feel that their lives are determined by a design, while others may feel that they can control their own destiny.

3. The speaker is asking whether the storm can really be conquered and questioning whether it is worthwhile to even try.

Connecting with the Novel

Answers will vary. All three poems contain elements of hopelessness and feelings of being bound by fate or by the forces of nature. Students who think that the fate of the characters in the novel is unavoidable may think that "Design" best reflects the tone; they may see Ethan as a person trapped like the moth. Others may see the lonely setting of the farm reflected in visual images of "Desert Places" or "Storm Fear."

■ The Snow Man

1. Responses will vary. Students will probably conclude that the snow man is the man referred to in the last stanza, the "listener, who listens in the snow."

2. Most students will decide that "one must have a mind of winter" means that one must be a person who can contemplate the dark coldness of that season without despair.

3. Interpretations may vary. Students should note that the echo of the word "nothing" creates a cold, lonely sound, that it is an effective word for painting both a visual and a verbal picture of emptiness.

4. Students may note that the mood of the poem is solemn and sad, that the tone is cold. Images of crusted, still pine trees and junipers frozen with ice paint an image of a cold, still, ungiving landscape. They support the statement in the last line that the speaker feels that he is alone in a lifeless winter.

Connecting with the Novel

Ethan has contemplated, and will contemplate, the cold hopelessness of winter in his life; he is a prisoner of winter. He has missed his chance for a happier life, or a "spring."

Answer Key *(cont.)*

■ The Stone Boy

> **READING CHECK**
>
> **a.** While Arnold and his older brother, Eugene, are picking peas, Arnold's gun goes off, and he accidentally kills his brother.
>
> **b.** Arnold goes over to his brother and calls his name. Then he goes on to pick peas.
>
> **c.** The sheriff says that the shooting is an accident but asks questions that make it clear that he has doubts about Arnold's behavior.

1. Arnold looks up to his brother, fears his criticism, and feels somewhat inadequate next to him. He is reminded of his brother's superior position as the older one and describes his brother's tallness and mature looks.

2. Students will probably recognize that Arnold is waiting for some word from his family that will give him the opportunity to explain and express his own sorrow. Since they are unable or unwilling to speak, silence does in fact divide them forever.

3. Most students will recognize that after the accident, Arnold becomes the Stone Boy of the title. He stops speaking, and he endures what is happening to him without defending himself.

4. Responses will vary, but students might explain that Arnold was in a state of shock and was not thinking or behaving normally. They might note that he seemed to be acting on the impulse of the moment. Some students might give his youth as an explanation.

Connecting with the Novel

The silence of the characters in the novel and in the story is a shared theme. No one is able to speak about his or her feelings or express his or her thoughts. Each character is bound up in his or her own unhappiness, unable to find comfort in the other. The story and novel also share a somber and hopeless mood; there is no hint in either of them that things will change or improve in any way.

■ *from Ethan Frome* as Fairy Tale

> **READING CHECK**
>
> **a.** "Snow White"
>
> **b.** Ethan is the prince, Zeena is the witch, and Mattie is Snow White.
>
> **c.** The lovers do not live happily ever after. The witch wins.

1. Mattie has an expressive face, black hair, red cheeks, and white skin. She brims with health, youth, and vitality, like Snow White. Zeena is thin, with prominent bones, colorless hair, a gaunt nose, and granite skin. (Note the image of stone hardness.)

2. Ethan associates images of nature with Mattie. She has hair like the moon, a voice like an enchanted glade; her hands are like birds, and her eyelashes like butterflies. According to the essay, those associations make Mattie valuable to Ethan, and he idealizes her.

3. Zeena's purpose, like that of the witch in the fairy tale, is to hurt young people and deprive them of hope and joy. She achieves that by separating them.

Connecting with Novel

Students may be reminded of a number of fairy tales that include a young, innocent maiden and a cruel older woman—"Cinderella" and "Sleeping Beauty" are the most obvious. To make the novel more like a fairy tale, students should realize they would have to write a happy ending to the novel.

■ The Hiltons' Holiday

> **READING CHECK**
>
> **a.** The Hiltons' son died.
>
> **b.** Mrs. Hilton says that it is too hot and she has made plans to visit an aunt.
>
> **c.** The judge knew Mr. Hilton's mother.

1. The judge sees them with pleasure and remembers the family with respect; the clerk in the store responds to the little girls positively and gives them a treat; the old man also treats Mr. Hilton with respect and remembers the past. The community values respectability and tradition over wealth and material things.

2. Mr. Hilton is deeply content with the day, comforted by the thought that he has seen people who remember his family and that he has provided a treat for the girls. The girls are tired and happy; they are satisfied with their day and eager to share it with their mother. Mrs. Hilton is happy to have them home. She recognizes that she has had a lonely day without them, but she is pleased that they had a fine day. We can infer that they are a loving family whose members find pleasure in making one another happy and that they can be pleased by the small pleasures of life.

3. Students may see a quiet future for the girls—one that is similar to the life that their parents live. Others may think that the interest that Susan Ellen shows in the outside world might mean a different, more adventurous future for her.

Connecting with the Novel

The Hiltons seem to love and respect each other. They share their love and concern for their children. They think of the past with sadness but without bitterness. The Fromes do not have children to love and do not love each other. They share nothing and cannot find any pleasure in the things around them. They do not look at the past or the future with any happiness.

■ *from* A Backward Glance

> ### READING CHECK
> The main idea of the 1922 introduction to the novel is to explain the structure of the novel and the use of the narrator. In *A Backward Glance,* Wharton reveals that she had long wanted to write a realistic account of New England farm life and tells how she came to write *Ethan Frome.*

1. According to Wharton, she chose the story-within-a-story framework because it dealt best with a dramatic climax, which occurred a generation after the tragedy of the accident. She chose the narrator because she wanted the story to come from someone who was not involved in the events of the main story.

2. Wharton says that *Ethan Frome* gave her joy to write because she had wanted to write a realistic novel about New England life, one that did not look at life through "rose-colored spectacles."

3. Mrs. Hale and Harmon Gow give two views of the story, each contributing as much as he or she is capable of understanding. It is up to the narrator to see it all.

■ *from* Edith Wharton: A Biography

> ### READING CHECK
> Lewis maintains that the story of Ethan's unhappy marriage was based on Edith Wharton's own marriage. He also cites the real-life sledding accident that Wharton read about as a source for the story.

1. Wharton shifted the sexes in creating her three fictional characters, she placed them in a rural setting, and she made the outcome of the story a hopeless one. In her own life, Wharton, a wealthy woman, was able to escape her unhappy marriage.

2. Most students will probably feel that the ending and the setting made the novel realistic.

Connecting with the Novel

Most students will find the final scene—Mattie paralyzed and Ethan trapped—pretty grim.

■ The Angry Winter

> ### READING CHECK
> a. The creator determined that man would not live forever.
> b. a rabbit
> c. The community has vanished.

1. The writer admires the fact that the rabbit, too, has survived alone in the storm, that he is beaten and worn but still going.

2. Responses will vary. A possible meaning is that man has survived terrible times but at a price—he will always carry with him the memories of the struggle and the knowledge of his own mortality.

Connecting with the Novel

Most students will see that Ethan, like the writer of the essay, must contemplate the desolation of his life and face the knowledge that there will be no escape until death comes.

Test

■ Part I: Objective Questions

1. T	**6.** a	**11.** d
2. F	**7.** c	**12.** b
3. F	**8.** b	**13.** a
4. T	**9.** d	**14.** c
5. F	**10.** a	**15.** c

■ Part II: Short-Answer Questions

16. The story of Ethan Frome's disabling accident is set in a frame narrative that opens and closes the novel. The inner story takes place twenty-four years earlier than the frame story.

17. Light in the form of sunlight and lamplight is associated with Mattie, who brings vitality and hope into Ethan's life. Darkness and lack of color are associated with Zeena, who kills Ethan's hope and joy at every turn.

18. Mattie has been orphaned and left penniless by her "dishonored" father. Zeena offers her board at the farm in return for help with the housework. Having few alternatives, Mattie is grateful to Zeena and fears being sent back to work among strangers.

19. Mattie is a delicate, dreamy young woman unfit for hard work but with a capacity for joy and ten-

derness and an appreciation of beauty that captivates the sensitive Ethan.

20. Ethan is hampered by poverty, bad weather, and family responsibilities brought about by illness and social and emotional deprivation.

21. Ethan is troubled by a conflict between his desire for personal happiness and his sense of responsibility for others. He also seems to struggle with an inertia or passivity that makes it hard for him to sustain decisive action.

22. Zeena claims that her worsening illness requires their hiring more efficient household help than Mattie can provide and that they cannot afford to keep Mattie and pay a hired girl. She probably is jealous of Ethan's feelings for Mattie.

23. Zeena comes to nurse the dying Mrs. Frome. Zeena becomes obsessed with her own health. Ethan and Mattie are permanently disabled in the sledding accident. No one recovers except Zeena, who takes up the role of nurse again after the accident. However, illness remains the center of her existence.

24. Ethan and Mattie decide to die together rather than be separated, but they fail to kill themselves and end up tied together inescapably, achieving neither a full life nor death.

25. Sweet-natured Mattie, now an invalid, has become cross and complaining, while Zeena, the former querulous patient, has become the caretaker.

■ Part III: Essay Questions

a. Students should provide examples from the text that support their interpretation, such as the narrator and other characters' opinions of Ethan, the circumstances confronting Ethan, and his response to those circumstances.

b. In addition to providing examples of symbols, such as the snow, the cat, and Zeena's pickle dish, students should interpret them and explain how Wharton uses them to convey her themes. (See the Literary Terms Worksheets in this study guide or the Elements of Literature textbook.)

c. Students will most likely point out how the winter setting reinforces the harshness and deprivation of Ethan Frome's material and emotional life. Like winter, Ethan is strong and tenacious, but there is a frozen quality to his nature that prevents him from holding on to the warmth life offers him.

d. Students' evaluations will vary. Some may assert that the frame story confuses the time of the setting and dilutes the drama of the main story. Some may find the first-person narrator artificial, preferring to have Ethan tell his own story. Others may say that the frame story excites readers' interest in how and why Ethan became disabled and that it would not be realistic for an inarticulate character like Ethan to tell his own story.

e. Responses will vary according to the theme chosen. Successful essays will cover the introduction of the theme, its development in characters, events, and symbols, and, finally, an interpretation of the refinement of the theme in the ending.

f. Successful essays will include an introduction of the theme, issue, or character in both *Ethan Frome* and the **Connections** and will trace related elements through both texts.

Notes

Notes

Notes

Notes

Notes

Notes

Notes

Notes

Notes

Notes